GODDESS OF THE UNIVERSE

BOOK THREE

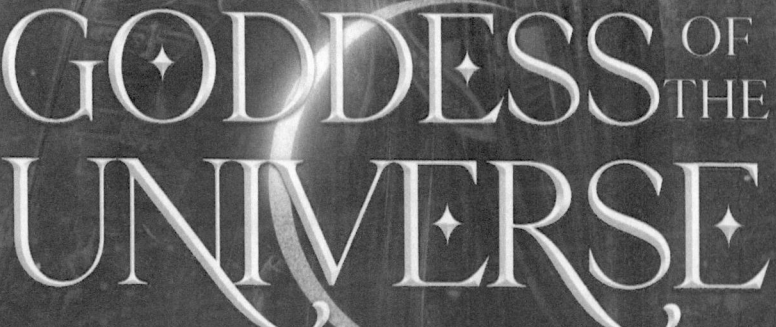

CATHERINE BANKS

GODDESS OF THE UNIVERSE

)3(

THEIR FAE GODDESS

Goddess of the Universe by Catherine Banks.

Cover design by Ana Cruz Arts.

Published by Turbo Kitten Industries.

www.CatherineBanks.com

Turbo Kitten Industries™, P.O. Box 5012, Galt, CA 95632

ACKNOWLEDGMENTS

Thank you to the following people who helped make this book possible:

C.R. for being such a fantastic person and helping me in ways she may never realize.

Lea for being awesome and helping me in so many ways.

Jenica for always being there. She means more to me than she knows.

As always, my amazing husband and best friend, Avery.

Thank you also to my amazing Kickstarter supporters:

Alicia Rades

Andromeda Taylor-Wallace

Annette McElroy

Betheny Thompson

Brooke

Candace Wondrak

Christina

Christina Hunt

Claire Ellison

Daniel Tice Jr

Derek Murphy

Helen Scott

Jacqueline Hayley

Jathan McBride

Kaiya Kagon

Jennifer Laslie

Jessica Paige

Jessica Robbins

Karri Allen

Altheda Rutherford

Kathy

Kristal Melton

Lance McKee

Leslie Twitchell

Marie Andreas

Mettie A.M.

Winter Bruno

Michael Green

Michelle McFarlin

Nikki Jefford

Sunny Side Up

Cali Mann

Rachel Strehlow

Shannon

Sky A Fallows

Stephanie Meier

Stuart March

Tanya

Wanda

Jaycee DeLorenzo

Anderelle

Zenlop

Minloa

Lilpo

Blustum

Menma

Dead Lands

Emortalia

Treska

Eltare

Distra

Olunce

Carnel

CHAPTER 1

ELARA

FOUR REDCAPS STOOD outside Daniel's house in Emortalia, hitting their clubs against their empty hands. It seemed they were trying to intimidate us with the display, but it wasn't working.

"Sit and watch," Durlan said and kissed my cheek. His long silver hair was pulled back and tied with a piece of leather. I preferred his hair free, but I also enjoyed the unblocked view of his handsome face.

I sat on Daniel's porch and tore into the dried meat Ryul had given me. "Okay," I said around the food.

Ryul sat beside me and chewed his meat.

Durlan, Amrynn, Venali, and Myrin walked away from the house, swords in hand.

Daniel leaned against the side of his house near me, his arms folded across his chest, and wore a bored expression.

"You could just let me have them all," Venali said, his magenta eyes glowing brightly with excitement.

"Not a chance," Durlan said, his hair whipping from side to side as he shook his head. "I need some exercise."

"There are other ways we can exercise," I called out loudly.

Durlan turned. "I plan on that after I've got you worked up from watching us kill these redcaps. Once we are done, I will take care of you."

He had been more aggressive lately, which I was pretty certain was due to the fact that he didn't have anything to strategize and was bored.

I was *not* complaining.

"Tease," I called back and took another bite.

He winked at me, and his sword began to glow.

Well, that was new.

"You underestimate us," the middle redcap growled. "It will be your downfall."

"We've killed at least twelve of your kind the past week," Venali said, still smiling, the three scars of his left eye slightly scrunched. "You underestimate us."

A few of the shapeshifters came out of their houses and sat on their porches like I did. They'd become desensitized to the redcaps' attacks and knew my guys could handle them.

If things started to get out of control, Daniel and Ryul would join the fight.

"Water?" Ryul asked and held out a cup.

I took it and guzzled it. "Thanks." I scooted a bit closer so I could lean my shoulder against his.

With the possibility of losing them so close, I was using every chance I had to touch them, spend time with them, and engage in whatever activities they wanted to. It resulted in several late nights where I ended up coated in sweat and smiling like a drunken fool, though no alcohol was present.

"Ready?" Myrin asked, smiling wide enough to show off

his sharp canines. Black tendrils slid from his fingertips, down his sword, and coated the blade. The blade glowed with a black sheen, and I wondered what it would feel like to get cut with it.

He leapt forward and sliced off one of the redcap's arms.

Judging by the way the redcap screamed, the sword hurt a lot more than a regular one.

Venali stopped, inhaled deeply, and the muscular Seelie became even more muscular. I had never seen muscles expand before, and it was quite the display.

The guys had begun using new powers, ones I had never seen them use while warlords. They said that the continued exposure to Amara, though small, was helping to unlock their suppressed powers. They said they were also trying out some new powers, to try to prepare for our upcoming battle.

I hoped there wouldn't be a battle, but the likelihood of that was very small. Infinitesimal really.

Venali roared and began punching the redcap in front of him. He had to jump up to hit the redcap in the face, since it was twice his height.

The redcap swung his club and tried to punch Venali back, but Venali dodged out of the way and blocked the punches with his arm.

Durlan moved forward slowly, his walk slow and confident. The redcap tried to hit him, but Durlan sidestepped his wild swings like the redcap was moving at a slower pace. Once right in front of the redcap, Durlan stabbed his glowing sword into the redcap's chest. It screamed and then exploded into a piercing white light.

"That's definitely new," I whispered and squeezed my legs together at the sudden rush of wetness between them.

Amrynn, who usually fought with his sword, sheathed it and took a Venali approach, fighting the redcap hand to hand. He pummeled it to death with ease.

Something was happening to them that they weren't telling me. They were all a bit angrier than before and way more focused on powering up. It wasn't just the upcoming fight. There was a rage simmering amongst them that none of them would talk about.

"It would be nice if at least one of you was honest about why you are all so angry," I whispered.

"It would be nice if you told us everything going on in your head, too," Daniel said.

Touché.

Myrin finished cutting up the redcap and used his black flames to destroy the bodies of the rest of the monsters.

All four men returned to the house, walking past me.

Well, that was over too quickly. Not that I was complaining that the god of darkness was sending tests that were too easy. I preferred them to ones that left us injured.

"Coming?" Ryul asked. He stood beside me with his hand extended in an offer to help me stand.

I took his hand and let him pull me up. My head spun a moment, and I grabbed his arm to keep steady.

He scowled down at me. "You've been practicing magic when we're sleeping, haven't you?"

I smiled innocently. "Me?"

He snarled. "You're going to hurt yourself by burning the candle at both ends."

"Why can't I work to become stronger just like you guys are?" I asked, stepping away from him now that the dizzy spell was over.

"I didn't say you couldn't become stronger. Just that you shouldn't do it under certain conditions. One: don't do it when we aren't with you, and two: you shouldn't use magic when you've already spent the entire day training physically," he said.

I walked into the house and headed to the bedroom where Durlan waited for me. "I'll take your advice into consideration."

Durlan yanked me into the bedroom and slammed the door closed.

I hopped up onto him, wrapping my legs around his waist, my arms around his neck, and kissed him.

He tugged at my shirt, and I broke the kiss to remove it.

He tossed me on the bed and took his own shirt off. "Now, let's see what we can do about you being able to walk properly."

I smirked. "I like this challenge. Bring it on, mate."

He smiled and dropped his pants, showing me just how ready he was for the challenge.

CHAPTER 2
AMRYNN

WE WERE PLANNING a trip to the one place on the planet I did not want to go, a continent full of violent humans. If they caught us, they'd either kill us or do as Barry had, and use us for experimentation.

Okay, I didn't know that for certain, but it was highly likely.

Sitting in the middle of the living room, Myrin and Venali allowed me to experiment on them. I stood at their backs while they sat, focused on my magic, and tried to channel it into Myrin's aura, to make him invisible.

I'd made Venali invisible several times, but I wasn't certain it would work on Myrin.

My magic swirled within his aura, his body began to fade, and then the darkness of his Unseelie power shoved my magic out, knocking Venali and I away from him.

I released my magic and snorted as I laughed.

Venali sat back up and shook his head. "Well, that was different."

Myrin sighed and hung his head. "I'm sorry. I come preprogrammed to reject Seelie powers."

I patted his shoulder. "My feelings aren't hurt."

He looked around and scowled. "Where's Elara?"

"She's with Daniel," I said and fought against my urge to snarl at him.

Myrin and Elara were connected in a different way than the rest of us. I couldn't figure out how it was different or why, but it bothered me. It bothered Kydrus as well, but we hadn't spoken to the others to ask if they felt the same.

I knew she loved us all equally, but there was a difference when they were together, and it was obvious.

"Amrynn?" Myrin asked.

I looked up, realizing I had spaced out again. "Sorry."

Venali gave me a knowing look, while Myrin scowled.

Daniel and her were connected differently as well, but not in a way that bothered me. I couldn't explain it even to myself, so I kept my feelings inside.

I knew there was no reason for me to be jealous. Elara loved me and would never leave me. Yet, my possessive brain still tried to convince me every now and then to scoop her up and run far far away with her.

I wouldn't do it, but thinking about it did bring a smile to my face.

"Try it with Venali again, so I can watch," Myrin said.

I nodded and turned to Venali. "It doesn't last long, though."

Myrin shrugged. "The fact that it works at all is interesting to me."

"Don't I get a say in this?" Venali asked.

I arched a brow at him.

"It feels weird," he mumbled.

I rolled my eyes. "Just sit still."

CHAPTER 3
ELARA

No ONE WAS willing to take us to Zenlop and the ship we had come here on wasn't sturdy enough for the rest of our trek. So, I had to purchase a ship to use instead. Thankfully, my mates knew how to sail so we wouldn't have to hire a crew.

Myrin checked the ship over thoroughly before paying the owner. "Sold," Myrin said.

The man smiled and walked away, counting his money.

"When do we set sail?" Durlan asked with a scowl.

He hadn't been able to come up with a plan that satisfied him, but I was tired of waiting. We needed to go now, before *he* made a move.

"Tomorrow," I said. "We'll need to check the stores and be sure we have enough food for the trip there and back."

"On it," Ryul said and walked onto the ship.

"You're sure this is necessary?" Amrynn asked.

I spun to face him since he'd stood off to the side. He was the least happy that we were going to the humans' continent. "Yes."

He sighed, but nodded. "I'll do some supply shopping."

I watched him go until he disappeared among the crowds of the dock.

"Elara, I have a really bad feeling about this," Venali said.

I sighed and dropped my head. "I understand this is dangerous. I understand you hate the idea of taking me somewhere so dangerous. If there were another way, Amara and I would gladly take it. As it is, there are two options. One, give myself to *him*..."

Venali, Myrin, Kydrus, Daniel, and Durlan growled.

"Or, two, I get this container. So, you tell me which you would prefer."

No one spoke.

"I thought so," I said.

"Doesn't mean we have to like it," Durlan growled.

I wrapped my arms around him, and he immediately enveloped me in a hug. "I don't like it either," I whispered.

"Daniel," Ryul called. "Come help me with the purchases, please."

Daniel dropped a kiss atop my head as he passed.

"I've got some adjustments to make before we set sail," Myrin said. "Venali and Kydrus, I'll need your help."

"What am I supposed to do?" I asked.

"Go rest," Myrin said. "You look exhausted."

Arguing would do me no good, especially since he was right.

Durlan looped an arm around my waist and tugged me away. "Come on."

He teleported us to Daniel's house and led me to the bedroom.

I flopped onto the bed, face down.

Durlan climbed on beside me and stroked my hair.

For a bit, I just enjoyed being petted.

"I'm scared," I whispered.

"Of?" Durlan asked, still petting me.

"Losing you all."

"We're scared of losing you, too," he whispered.

He didn't understand that I meant losing him once Amara separated from me.

Was he afraid of losing me or Amara?

"I love you, Durlan," I whispered. "I want to do whatever I can to protect you." Even if it meant sacrificing myself or my happiness.

He turned me over and kissed away the few tears that had escaped. "You're hiding something from us. We all know it. We can all feel the difference in you since the day *he* came. I wish you would talk to us."

"It's not a secret," I said. "Just possibilities that I'm preparing for."

"Like us dying?" he asked.

I nodded. *Among others.*

"I can't promise that I won't die," he whispered. "But I can promise to try my hardest to live."

Except if his life could be traded for mine, he'd break that promise.

"Amara and I merged a bit more," I whispered. "It's becoming hard to know where Elara ends and Amara begins."

He stroked my face. "We love you both, so it doesn't bother us."

"She...we love you," I whispered.

"What aren't you telling us?" he asked softly.

"I...can't."

"Can't or won't?" he asked, his voice still gentle.

I didn't answer.

He sighed. "Go to sleep, Elara. You need the rest. Tomorrow is the start of a new adventure."

I snuggled up close to him and closed my eyes.

Instantly, I stood before a mirror with Amara glaring at me.

"What?" I asked and put my hands on my hips.

"You almost told him," she accused.

"I didn't, though," I snapped back.

"We're merging more," she whispered. "I hadn't anticipated this."

"What does that mean?" I asked.

"If we fully merge, I'm not sure I can separate us."

I gaped at her. "You said you're a goddess, so of course you could do it."

"That was before we merged more," she said and waved her hands frantically. "I thought I had stopped it, but clearly fate has other ideas."

"Maybe it's a good thing," I said softly.

She smirked. "So, we get our cake and eat it, too?"

I nodded.

"When you get to Zenlop, disguise yourself as a human. You'll have to break into the museum. Make—"

"Ryul use his magic on the guards so we can take the item right under their noses," I finished.

She nodded.

"I've got it," I said. "I just don't know how we'll get to the docks."

She smiled. "Leave that to me."

I didn't like that smile. That was our crazy idea smile.

CHAPTER 4
KYDRUS

"Do we even know how long the journey will take?" I asked Myrin as I held a wooden beam and he nailed it in.

"A few days was all I was told," Myrin said. He pounded the nail in and then added a second.

"Wonderful," I murmured.

Sweat beaded on my forehead as I continued to hold up the beam. It was hot below deck and incredibly stuffy.

Myrin finally finished securing the beam and grabbed another one.

"What are we building?" I asked.

"A room for Elara," he said. "I don't want her alone in the captain's quarters, or with just one of us."

I liked his plan.

"Good idea," I said.

Venali carried over more beams and some panels. "This should be it," he said and dusted off his hands.

Myrin nodded and placed the next beam. "Here."

Venali held it in place this time.

"What are we going to do about a bed?" I asked.

"I figured we could steal Daniel's since he's coming with us," Myrin said and smiled. "It holds on to her smell, even when she's not on it."

"I think we should leave Amrynn on the boat when we land," I whispered.

Myrin stopped his hammer, letting it fall to his side. "I was going to suggest it, but thought he would argue."

"He will," I said with a smirk. "He will also do as we tell him. We just have to be persuasive."

"I'll leave you to do it then," Myrin said with a wide smile and turned back to securing the beam.

I growled, but accepted my fate. "Jerk."

Myrin laughed, as did Venali.

"What do you want to bet that she's not sleeping but strategizing with Amara?" Myrin said.

Venali chuckled. "No one will take that bet because that's a given."

"You still think Amara will try to separate from Elara?" I asked Myrin.

Myrin's hammer hit the nail harder than usual and he growled. "Yes. I guarantee that is one of the options they are considering."

"That's why Elara is acting differently?" Venali asked.

Myrin growled again. "I'm not sure. They put up walls so thick I cannot break through. And Elara has been swinging back and forth so much that I can't get a read on her."

CHAPTER 5
ELARA

I woke with Durlan reading in bed with me, and the house silent.

"No one's back?" I asked as I sat up.

Durlan shook his head and closed the book he had been reading. "How do you feel?" he asked, smoothing down my hair.

Always the worrier of the group.

I smiled and leaned forward to kiss him. "I'm fine."

His eyes burned with hunger, and he rolled on top of me, sliding his hand up beneath my shirt to stroke my breast.

I gasped and arched into him, but there were blankets between us.

He growled and tossed the blankets off the bed and then pulled his erection free.

I was trapped beneath him, so I couldn't take my underwear off.

He tugged my underwear to one side and slid a finger inside of me, checking how wet I was. He moaned as it slid in easily. "You've been extra wet lately."

"I keep watching you kill redcaps," I said, my lower body coiled with anticipation.

He slid into me, both of us moaning at the same time. He reached up and gripped my hair, tugging firmly, but not painfully. "You like it when I'm rough?" he asked.

I gasped and breathed, "Yes."

He slammed into me hard, our skin slapping together. "You like when I'm in charge?"

"Yes," I moaned as he thrust in and out of me.

He flipped me over, grabbed my hair in his fist, and pulled me back so that I was sitting up on my knees, my throat bent to the side, while he was still inside me. Had he been shorter, this position wouldn't have worked.

Growling, he pressed his canines to my throat and licked. "You tell me if I go too far, okay?" he whispered.

I nodded.

His teeth pressed harder. "Use your words."

"Yes," I said, trying to rock my hips, but he dropped a hand to grab them.

Starting a fast rhythm, he brought me to climax again and again. Then, when I was sure I couldn't possibly have more, he bit my neck and groped my breasts.

A scream tore from my throat as the mother of all orgasms hit. I felt my own juices leak down the inside of my legs as my thighs quivered.

Durlan orgasmed a moment later and released my neck.

I fell onto my stomach, a contented mush pile.

Durlan disappeared and returned with a bandage. "I'm sorry," he whispered as he wiped my neck.

"Durlan, I'm fine," I said.

"You're bleeding," he whispered.

I was?

I grabbed his hand and made him look at me. "I enjoyed every second of that. Okay? Don't apologize for making me feel good."

He smiled and kissed me. "Okay."

After he bandaged my neck, I went to the bathroom to clean up.

That was a new side of Durlan I hadn't seen before.

I smiled at my reflection.

I could definitely get used to that side being around.

CHAPTER 6

RYUL

I STARED out at the ocean, water as far as I could see. Even knowing how to swim now, it scared me. I didn't like being scared.

"You'll be fine," Venali said from behind me.

I jumped. For such a large man, he moved silently.

"I don't like not being near land," I said, turning to face him.

He had a large sack on his shoulder, but stood loosely like it weighed nothing to him. "I don't like it either," he said. He shrugged, making the sack move. "But we have no choice."

Part of me wanted to ask to carry the sack to see if it was light, but I didn't want to be unable to lift it if it was heavy.

"What's in the bag?" I asked.

He glanced at the bag on his shoulders. "Potatoes."

Amrynn walked onto the ship with a bag over his shoulder. "How's it going?" he asked.

"We're almost done," Venali said.

I nodded my agreement.

Amrynn nodded and headed below deck.

Venali followed.

With nothing else to do, I followed as well.

They had transformed a huge portion of the area into a room, though no bed was there yet.

"You guys work fast." I smiled at their work.

Myrin beamed. "Thanks."

"We ready to head back?" I asked.

"I'm going to stay on the ship to guard it," Amrynn said.

Myrin nodded. "Great. We'll be back in just a few hours."

"Hours?" I asked.

"I want us to sleep on the ship tonight," Myrin said. "So we can get used to it before we set sail."

I guessed that made sense.

Kydrus sat against a wall of the new room. "I'll just stay here."

Amrynn chuckled. "Out of shape, old friend?"

"I'll still whip you in the ring." Kydrus snarled. Then he sighed. "But yes."

Daniel approached, having been in the storage area. "We done?"

"We're going to the house for a bit," Venali said. "We need to collect our mate."

Daniel looked at the room. "And steal my bed?"

Myrin smiled. "Is it stealing if you'll be using it, too?"

Daniel chuckled and pushed his way through, heading to the stairs. "Let's go. I don't want to leave her alone too long."

"She does attract trouble like a magnet," I said.

Kydrus smiled. "You don't know the half of it."

Sudden pain engulfed my mind.

Elara! She's in trouble.

Everyone crowded together, and Amrynn teleported us to Daniel's house.

Elara stood outside the house, Durlan on the ground beside her, not moving. Before her, three Cu Sith snarled and snapped their jaws. They were huge, black dogs with shadows flickering along their shaggy fur.

I had never seen Cu Sith before, but there were dozens of tales about them. They were supposedly harbingers of death, collectors of souls.

"Come closer, and I will kill you," Elara hissed through her teeth as she snarled at them. "You will not take my mate's soul."

The middle Cu Sith barked.

Elara cried out in pain and dropped to one knee. "No," she yelled. Her body began glowing, but she only raised one hand. The other had blood dripping down it.

Daniel shifted into his bear form and roared.

The rest of us drew our swords and charged forward, putting ourselves between Elara and the Cu Sith.

Amrynn stepped back and knelt by Durlan. "He's alive. Unconscious. Seriously wounded."

Elara's entire body trembled. "They were trying to take his soul," she whispered. "They were sent by *him*."

That much I had figured.

Myrin's darkness swirled around him, and he bared his teeth at the Cu Sith. "Leave now or we'll destroy you."

Daniel growled and stood on his hind legs, now over eight feet tall.

I would never admit it to him, but he was pretty intimidating.

The Cu Sith on the left growled.

Elara growled back. "You're not fully immortal. Even gods die, and so will you."

"You understand them?" I asked, keeping my eyes on the enemy.

"Yeah. Part of Amara's powers I think," she whispered.

The three Cu Sith leapt at Daniel, jaws snapping and claws bared.

Myrin kicked one in the side, sending it flying into a tree.

Daniel swatted another one away, his massive paw as powerful as our fists.

Venali grabbed the third by the throat and slammed it to the ground in front of Daniel.

The two that had been sent flying leapt up and charged back.

I sliced across the front leg of the one nearest to me, my sword cutting to the bone.

Turning, it tried to clamp its jaws on my arms, but I stepped left and tried to stab it in the chest.

The Cu Sith dropped to the ground, avoiding my strike.

Venali cut the head off the Cu Sith he was fighting, and then Myrin set it on fire with his black flames.

Spinning my magic, I used it on the Cu Sith facing me. He tensed and looked around with wide eyes.

With three swings, I decapitated it and pierced its heart.

"Myrin," I called.

He turned, raised his hand, and black flames covered the Cu Sith at my feet.

His flames were *really* useful.

The last Cu Sith snarled and backed up, looking like he was planning to flee.

Myrin rushed forward, grabbed it by the scruff, and

flames engulfed it. "No one hurts my mate and lives," he growled and tossed the burning canine to the forest floor.

Daniel shifted back and tried to examine Elara's wounds, but she brushed his hands away.

Amrynn was still healing Durlan, a scowl on his face that made me uneasy.

Elara dropped to the ground by Durlan, tears streaking her cheeks, and then leaned forward to press her lips to his.

"Live," Amara's voice said from Elara's throat.

White energy floated from Elara to Durlan, sliding into his mouth.

When the last bit of energy left her mouth, Elara fell backwards on the forest floor, eyes closed.

Durlan sat up and looked around with wide eyes. He looked at Elara and reached over, resting his hand on her chest bone. A second later, he exhaled harshly. "Elara, you moron." He looked up at us. "What happened?"

"The Cu Sith are dead," Myrin said and indicated their burning corpses. "You tell us what you remember, and we'll fill you in."

Durlan picked up Elara's completely limp form. He noticed my worry and said, "She's alive. Though right now I want to kill her."

"How did she heal you?" Amrynn asked, standing with fists clenched at his sides.

Durlan turned and carried Elara into the house, ignoring the question.

We followed.

He set her on the couch, glaring at her.

Why was he mad at her? What had that white energy been?

"Durlan," Amrynn growled.

"I didn't ask her to do it," he snapped and bared his teeth at Amrynn. "I never would have asked that of her."

"Durlan," Myrin said softly.

He exhaled loudly and ran a hand through his hair. Or, attempted to, but there were tangles and debris that hindered his move. "She gave me part of her life force. Elara shortened her life to heal me."

"By how much?" I asked, my heart hammering in my chest.

"I don't know!" Durlan yelled. "This damn Seelie woman just doesn't listen. We're supposed to protect her, not the other way around. Why did Amara even agree?" He plopped down on the floor and put his face in his hands.

Daniel examined her wounds and scowled at her neck. "Why is there a bandage here?"

"That happened before the Cu Sith showed up," Durlan mumbled. "Don't ask."

Daniel tore her shirt open so he could clean her wounds. There were several cuts on her shoulder and chest, likely claw marks from the Cu Sith.

Amrynn said, "I'm going to the ship."

Kydrus set his hand on his shoulder. "Me, too."

No one missed the fierce expression on Amrynn's face. I just couldn't understand why he wore it. We were all shocked and upset, but it was hardly Durlan's fault.

"Let's finish packing and get back to the ship," Myrin said. "The sooner we leave, the better."

Durlan stood suddenly and loomed over Elara. "Amara," he growled. "Get out here, right now."

Elara's eyes opened, their color changing to Amara's.

"Don't be angry," Amara said softly. "She wanted to save you and this was the only way."

"How could you let her do that?" Durlan snapped. "You know I wouldn't want that."

Amara smiled. "She loves you. She had other reasons, which she used to convince me."

"Like what?" Durlan asked and folded his arms across his chest.

"I won't reveal that. If she wishes to, she will, but I doubt it," Amara said.

"How much did she give me? How much of her life did she lose to heal me?" Durlan asked.

Everyone tensed, waiting for the answer.

"Do you really want to know?" she asked. "What will knowing benefit you or her?"

"I need to know," Durland said, his voice soft. "Please."

"Two hundred years," Amara said.

I fell onto the chair behind me. The others looked as stricken as I was.

Durlan stormed out of the house, not even shutting the door on his way out.

Venali left, too, I hoped he was going to follow after Durlan.

"She'll sleep for two days," Amara said. "Let her rest and don't be hard on her." She looked at Myrin. "She did what her heart felt was right. Don't punish her for that."

Myrin nodded. "Okay."

She smiled. "Don't fret, my loves. She and I have a plan."

"That you won't tell us," I guessed.

Her eyes stopped glowing and closed.

Amara had left.

"Anyone else convinced Elara is planning to sacrifice herself?" I asked, a lump in my throat at the thought of losing her.

No one answered me, but I knew the answer.

Now the question was, how to prevent it?

CHAPTER 7

ELARA

I REALLY HAD TO PEE, but I knew when I opened my eyes, I would have to face seven angry mates. One who was going to be *super* mad.

My bladder rebelled, and I was forced to sit up. I was on Daniel's bed, but we were not in his house.

I held still, let my senses adjust, and took everything in.

Wood creaked. The ground swayed gently. Water crashed nearby.

Ship. We were on the ship.

I slid out of bed and walked until I found what served as a restroom.

Once done, I headed for the stairs that led to the top of the ship where everyone likely was. Nervous, I froze at the bottom of the stairs.

What was I going to say to them? To him?

"Best to get it over with," Myrin said behind me.

I yelped and spun around.

He looked sad, which was not the reaction I had expected.

"I'm not sorry," I said. "I'd do it again...for any of you."

Myrin nodded. "We know."

I frowned. "You're not mad at me?"

He chuckled, but there was no mirth in it. "I'm furious, but yelling at you won't do either of us any good."

I wasn't sure I preferred this to yelling.

"Go on," Myrin urged. "You can't hide here forever."

I could try.

With a resigned sigh, I walked up the stairs and into the fading sunlight, shielding my eyes from it.

"You're awake," Daniel said. "How does your shoulder feel?"

I looked at my shapeshifter mate, his rounded ears peeking out of his hair and smiled. "Fine."

He didn't return my smile, just nodded and resumed carving a piece of wood.

At the front of the ship, Durlan stood, arms folded, looking out at the water.

Taking a breath for courage, I walked to him and stood at his side, looking out at the waves.

He dropped his arms to his sides, then dropped to the ground in a bow.

I turned, mouth agape. "Wh—"

"I failed you. I failed to protect you. By rights, you should cast me out. I deserve no less."

"You didn't fail me. You're not going anywhere. Amara needs you," I choked on a lump in my throat. "I need you."

He didn't move.

"Stand, please," I said.

He stood, but wouldn't look at me.

"Are you going to ignore me the rest of my life?" I asked.

"If you want to yell at me, that's okay. I won't apologize, though."

"Why are you so carefree with your life?" he asked, looking up at me with a pained expression. "Why don't you value it?"

I rested my hand on his chest, over his fast beating heart. "I'm a Seelie girl. Raised a slave. Queen by blood. I have one goal, one reason for being important. That is as Amara's vessel. I am here to help defeat the dark god. Then..." Exhaling loudly, I continued. "Then, my usefulness to Amara is over. The Seelie need righting, but whether it is me or another who does it, is not important." I gripped his chest lightly. "Keeping you alive to help Amara, keeping you alive is what is important. I'll give up every year of my life to keep you alive to be with Amara."

He pulled me forward, crushing me against his body. "I want you to live. I want to see you smiling and laughing a thousand years from now. You are important. You are important to me...to them." He jerked his head over mine, and I turned, all of the others stood nearby. "You do not have to sacrifice yourself. We don't want you to sacrifice yourself. There must be another way. There *has* to be another way."

I pushed away from him, tears forming in my eyes. "You don't understand."

"Explain it, then," he yelled. "Why do you have to sacrifice yourself?"

"Because I'd rather die than live my life without you," I yelled back. I clapped a hand over my mouth, eyes wide.

Crap. I hadn't meant to say that out loud.

I ran to the captain's cabin and locked the door behind me.

Crap. Crap. Crap. What had I just done?

"You're going to have to face them," Amara whispered in my mind.

"I can stay in here until we get to our destination," I said.

"Just tell them," she said with a sigh.

The door to the cabin groaned and then was pulled completely off its hinges and tossed across the deck.

Daniel stood in the open doorway, dusting off his hands. "Much better."

I glared at him.

He stalked inside, grabbed me, and tossed me over his shoulder.

"Hey," I yelled and tried to get free.

A warm palm slapped my butt. "Quiet."

My eyes widened. He'd spanked me.

He carried me out to the deck where the others were, set me on a barrel, and folded his arms across his chest. "Explain yourself," he said.

"We're running out of options," I said. "Amara and I merged more, which wasn't supposed to happen. At the end of this, we'll have two choices: separate or merge. But it depends on how things go against the dark god. We may not have a choice."

Myrin's eyes hardened. "Amara is considering giving herself to him, isn't she?"

I nodded. "She'd separate from me if she does that. That's our last resort option."

"You have your own plan that involves sacrificing yourself," Amrynn said, his silver hair blowing in the wind.

I nodded again. "I do. It might be the only way to save you all and Amara."

All seven growled.

Folding my arms across my chest, I held their glares. "I'm preparing for worse case scenarios. I don't want to die, but I know it's possible."

"We won't let you," Amrynn growled. "I won't let you sacrifice yourself."

Shrugging, I hopped off the barrel. "You'll try, but I have plan for that, too."

"Why don't you share these plans with us?" Durlan asked.

"Because you'll try to come up with a plan to stop me," I said and rolled my eyes. "Let's focus on the current problem. Getting the container."

A creature ran across the deck.

"What?" I yelled.

A tiny goblin. It had something shiny in its hand.

My crown.

"It has my crown," I yelled and ran after it. Where did it think it was going to go?

The guys ran after it. Kydrus teleported in front of it, but the goblin veered left.

Myrin tried to grab it, but it suddenly disappeared.

My mouth hung open.

"Why would a goblin steal her crown?" Durlan asked.

"Where could it have gone?" Daniel asked, lifting his nose to try to find its scent.

I dropped to my butt on the deck. My crown, with Barry's universe, was gone.

"He took it," I whispered, numb.

Venali rested his hand on my head. "I'm sorry," he whispered.

Durlan had made the crown for me, the day we agreed to be mates.

I was fairly certain no one could do anything with the planets in it, but the fear of Barry being freed hit me a second.

Amrynn knelt in front of me. "It'll be okay. We know what type of technology they have and won't be caught off guard if he somehow happens to escape. I don't think he will, though."

Tears welled in my eyes. If I did live, I planned to cherish the crown for its sentimental value. It would remind me of them even when they were gone. Now, I had nothing from them.

"I can make you a new crown," Durlan said softly.

Why did everything always have to become so complicated? Couldn't the universe throw me a bone?

The ship was eerily quiet, all of our moods soured as we continued to sail. The moon rose as night set and the moon and stars shone above us, giving us light to see. The guys moved about robotically, taking care of the ship without uttering a single sound.

I thought I might go crazy with all the quiet, when Ryul began singing a song my mother had sung to me as a child. It was a story of a warrior sent to battle, his children and wife left behind. It ended happily, but was sad for most of it.

His voice carried on the wind, seeming to spread everywhere.

I joined in, my voice melding with his.

As the last lyric faded into the night, I closed my eyes and breathed in the salty ocean air.

Someone started singing a new song, their voice deep and melodic. I opened my eyes and barely stopped from gasping.

I'd had no idea Venali was such a beautiful singer.

Amrynn and Kydrus joined in on the song and then so did Durlan.

Theirs was a lively song, one that sounded like a marching song.

Venali pulled me to my feet and spun us around the deck in a fast dance while he continued to sing.

As soon as that song ended, they sang another. They took turns dancing with me, and by the time we all panted from the exertion, we were all smiling.

If they went with Amara and I lived, I would never find men who could replace them. They were perfect.

Leaning my elbows on the railing, I watched the water sliced through by the ship.

What lay beneath the waves? Were there creatures with as much sentience as us?

"Come to bed," Myrin called.

I turned around and then quickly spun back around as something shiny darted by the boat. I searched for sight of it again, but either I had imagined it, or it was gone.

"You see something?" Myrin asked from behind me.

"Not sure," I muttered.

He took my hand and tugged. "Venali's on watch. If there's something, he'll alert us."

Venali blew me a kiss from the ship's helm.

I pretended to catch it and put it in my pocket.

Myrin chuckled and tugged me below and to our bed.

Amrynn and Kydrus were already under the covers, snoring softly.

I sat on the bed and Myrin pulled my boots off for me.

Crawling slowly, I made my way to the pillows, trying not to disturb my sleeping mates.

I had just started to wiggle beneath the covers when Myrin flung them back.

"I was trying not to wake them," I whispered.

"They woke up as soon as you got on the bed," Myrin said.

Kydrus pulled me down and spooned himself around me. "He's right."

Nestled in his arms, I expected to fall asleep quickly, but sleep continued to evade me.

"You're fidgeting," Myrin said.

"Am not," I whispered.

"Are too," Kydrus said around a yawn.

"Sorry," I sighed.

CHAPTER 8

DANIEL

"She's so infuriating," Ryul growled as he paced across the deck.

Venali steered the ship and kept an eye out from the helm. We didn't need to be awake or out here, but we all felt it was better to have multiple people on watch, rather than just one of us. Plus, although the bed was large enough for us to share, it was nice when there were only two other males in it with Elara.

"She loves you guys. She doesn't want to live without you. I can understand that. I don't want to live without Amara," I said.

Ryul stopped pacing and looked at me, a fierce expression on his face. He took a breath and shook his head. "I keep forgetting that you haven't been around since we met Elara, so you don't know her as well."

That wasn't completely true. I did know her. I did care for her. I just wasn't in love with her like I was in love with Amara. I knew they were connected, but there was a bit of separation between them.

"Would you leave if Amara ceased to exist and it was only Elara?" Venali asked.

I sighed and dropped my head to look back at the carving in progress in my hand. "I don't know."

"She loves you," Venali said. "She can't separate her love for you from Amara."

I nodded. That much I knew.

"She'd be devastated if you left," Ryul said softly.

"I didn't say I would leave for sure," I grumbled.

"We just have to keep them from dying or separating," Venali said. "Easy peasy."

I let out a bark of laughter.

Ryul sighed and sat in front of me. "How are we going to accomplish that? How are we going to keep her from sacrificing herself? She already gave up two centuries of her life for Durlan."

"Don't look at me," I mumbled. "I can't even figure out how to get her to sleep when she's supposed to."

"I sleep when I'm tired," Elara said.

We all spun to look at her as she walked up onto the deck.

She was beautiful, but when the moonlight hit her, it highlighted her cheekbones and made her gorgeous.

Walking with her head raised, staring up at the moon, she made her way to us. Her arms were out a bit, her hands splayed, but I couldn't figure out why.

"If you looked where you were going, you wouldn't have to keep your hands out to avoid bumping into things," Ryul said.

She dropped her head, stuck her tongue out at him, and then raised her face to the moon again. "It's so bright tonight. Full and beautiful."

Venali darted down from the helm, picked her up, and carried her back to the helm where he hugged her against him. "You're beautiful."

Her cheeks reddened, and she smiled. "You're such a sweet talker. How did one of the most deadly males I know become so smooth with women?"

He averted his gaze, acting like he was checking the other direction. "Only sweet for you, my love."

She scoffed and pushed away from him. "Liar." Turning her back, she walked to the edge of the ship and leaned against the railing. "Do we know if there are any sentient creatures in the waters?"

"There are giant sea serpents who are quite intelligent," Venali said. "There are also some other beings who I have heard of, but have never seen."

"How large is a giant sea serpent?" she asked, a little quiver to her lower lip.

"Four times the length of the ship," he said.

Her mouth dropped open, and she spun to face him. "Are you serious? No, you have to be pulling my leg."

"I'm serious," he said. "You don't have to worry about them, Elara. We'll kill them before they hurt you."

"I'm worried about the ship," she said. "How would we get home if they destroyed the ship?"

"We'd have to repair the ship," Venali said.

She edged away from the railing with wide eyes. "What other creatures are out there that I haven't seen?"

"A lot," I said.

She glanced at me. "You've been awfully quiet the last few days. You okay?"

I nodded, resuming my carving.

"What are you carving?" she asked, coming to stand beside me.

"Not really sure yet," I said.

Ryul pulled her down into his lap and kissed her cheek. "Why aren't you sleeping?"

"I couldn't sleep, and I was keeping the others awake," she said.

"Fidgeting?" Ryul asked.

"I do *not* fidget," she grumbled.

"You totally fidget," Ryul said.

She stuck her tongue out at him, and he grasped it with his thumb and finger.

She yelped and tried to pull back, but he held on.

"I told you that I'd grab your tongue if you kept sticking it out at me," he whispered with a victorious smile.

"Let go," she said as he continued to hold it.

"Not until you say the magic words," he said.

"Ryul's a butt," she mumbled.

He tickled her side, making her squeal and thrash. "Say it."

"I'll never surrender," she said as she laughed and struggled against him.

He released her and kissed her cheek. "You're crazy."

"Crazy for seven crazy men," she said and looked up at me with a wide smile.

I wanted to return her smile, but couldn't.

Her smile slipped and she stood, pain etched in her features.

I'd done that. I had caused her pain.

"I'll try to go to sleep," she said in a soft voice, heading back towards the stairs.

Ryul looked at me, and I could feel Venali's eyes on me as well.

As much as I wanted to go to her, to end the pain I had caused, I just continued my carving.

"What was that about?" Ryul asked, standing with a scowl.

"That's between me and her," I said.

"She doesn't know what is going on between you two either, though," Venali said.

I looked up at him. "She said something to you?"

He shook his head. "No, but I can tell. She's hurt because she doesn't know why you're suddenly pushing her away."

There was a crash and then Elara yelled out in pain.

The three of us raced down the stairs.

Elara lay at the bottom of the stairs, body splayed out on the ground and her eyes closed.

"Elara," Ryul yelled and ran to her, checking her. "She's breathing."

The scent of her blood hit me, making me snarl. "She's bleeding."

Ryul looked her over and shook his head. "There are no wounds."

Crap. That was a bad sign.

I walked down to her and sniffed around her body, freezing and tensing when I found the scent in her head. "She's bleeding in her head."

"Wake up Durlan," Venali snapped.

Ryul dashed away.

I cradled her head in my lap and stroked her hair.

Was this my fault? Had she fallen because of the tears streaking her face?

Durlan dropped down beside her and looked at me.

"She's bleeding in her head," I said.

Durlan's eyes widened, and he reached out, pressing his hand to her forehead. Warm light glowed from his hand and covered her head.

A few tense moments later, which I wasn't certain whether I had breathed during, her eyelids fluttered open, and she looked up at Durlan.

"What happened?" she asked.

"You fell down the stairs," Ryul said.

She sat up, and I quickly backed away and stood.

She rubbed at her head. "Oh. I feel like an idiot."

"You need to be careful," Durlan said, giving me a side eye.

"You were bleeding in your head," I said from my new position away from her.

She glanced at me, but quickly averted her eyes. "Sorry to have bothered you," she said, her voice wavering. With slow movements, she stood and headed towards her room.

Durlan stood and arched a brow. "Want to talk about it?"

"He won't even talk to her about it," Ryul said.

I growled. "Mind your own business, boy."

"Boy? I'm over a thousand years older than you," he scoffed and his body tensed.

I hadn't fought against Ryul, but if he attacked me, I wouldn't hold back.

"What's going on?" Myrin asked, coming from the bedroom and stood between us.

I turned and headed back to the deck. "Nothing you need to concern yourself with," I said.

I took over at the helm, since Venali wasn't there.

"You know you can talk to me," Myrin said. "I'm in a similar situation as you."

"You're not sure about her either?" I asked.

He chuckled. "Oh, I'm sure of her, but I've been around her longer. Elara doesn't take long to worm her way into your heart."

"Why couldn't Amara just take her over, like we did with our bodies?" I asked. "It would have made things so much easier."

"Since when has Amara done anything to make things easy?" Myrin asked.

I laughed bitterly. Too right he was.

"Look, you may not be sure about her or any of this, but could you try to go easier on her? She loves you and she doesn't know what to do when you treat her like that. She's young and inexperienced, but her heart is big and she loves with all of it."

"It's not like I hate her or anything," I mumbled.

"She thinks you do," he said.

I spun and gaped at him. "What?"

"She thinks you hate her now. She said she doesn't know what she did wrong, but you are mad at her and hate her and she doesn't know how to fix it because whenever you look at her, she just feels awful and wants to cry," he said.

"She said that?" I asked, an eyebrow arched.

He nodded. "When she came to bed just now. She was in hysterics. Amrynn and Kydrus are calming her down."

I ran a hand through my hair and sighed. "I didn't mean to upset her that much. I don't hate her. I just don't love her like you guys do."

"She's extremely emotional. This entire plan has her on

edge, and she's trying to forget that she plans to sacrifice herself and enjoy the little bit of time she has with us before she dies. You're making that hard for her when you're treating her like a stranger."

He held up his hand, stopping me from responding.

"I'm not saying to lie to her or just pretend everything is okay. Just talk to her. She'll understand," he said. He exhaled and asked, "Do you want me to take over so you can get some sleep? I don't think I'll be going to sleep anytime soon."

I shook my head at the thought of going down where she was. "No."

"You can't hide from her forever. You're on a ship together," he chuckled.

"I know," I growled.

He patted my shoulder. "Just think about what I said. She's a sweet girl and none of this is her fault. She didn't want any of this anymore than we did."

I nodded. "I got it. I understand what you're saying."

He nodded and walked away.

At first, I had thought she was fully Amara, just with memory loss or something. The more time I spent with her, the more I realized how different they were. Elara wasn't Amara and I loved Amara, had for centuries. It felt wrong to love another woman, even if she was the vessel. Even if the others loved her.

CHAPTER 9
KYDRUS

I HAD FINALLY GOTTEN her to fall asleep, her head on my chest.

Knowing that she'd had a bleed in her brain worried me and kept me from sleeping.

"Want a break?" Ryul asked as he climbed in bed.

I shook my head. "Just got her to sleep."

He nodded and lay down beside her. "I didn't even know she was hurt," he whispered. "If it weren't for Daniel..." He let his words trail off.

Durlan would have sensed it when he went to heal her, but it was worrisome that she had hurt herself so much.

Part of me wanted to punch Daniel in the face, but I did understand how he felt. I couldn't say I felt the same, because I had loved Elara since we had lived in Linta, but I could understand.

"Don't be hard on him," I whispered to Ryul.

Ryul scoffed and closed his eyes. "Whatever. If they separate, it just means one less man warming her bed with me."

My eyes widened. "So, you've chosen?"

"I had no choice. Elara has been my love for centuries. That's not going to change now. I love Amara, too, but Elara is my childhood friend and first love."

"Any ideas on what she might be planning?" I asked. Of us all, I hoped he might know something.

He sighed and shook his head. "No. I'm trying to think about what she could want or plan to do, but I can't."

"If you think of anything, let us know, okay?" I asked.

Elara stirred, nestling her head on my chest and sighing as her skin rubbed against mine. "Kydrus," she whispered in her sleep.

My heart swelled at the sweet sound of my name on her lips. The love she conveyed in that one word was beyond measure.

Ryul and I stopped talking and just watched her sleep.

"Someday, I'm going to kill that asshole who haunts her and we're going to live happily ever after," Ryul whispered.

I chuckled. "Let's hope so. First, we have to figure out how to deal with the humans we are headed towards."

He nodded. "I know. Apparently, Amara has a plan for us to get past their defenses and get on the island. Amara hasn't even told Elara the plan, though. That worries me more than anything else."

That worried me, too. What could Amara have planned that could get us past their defenses and to land without being seen or destroyed?

From what I had heard, no one made it to land. No one made it close without being blown up.

Would she cause a distraction somewhere else to draw attention away? Or would our crazy goddess do something else?

CHAPTER 10

ELARA

THE DAY HAD BEEN QUIET, and then a cannonball landed near the ship, making the water spray up over me.

Two more feet and I would have been hit by it.

"Pirates," Venali yelled, excitement in his voice.

"Stay near the mast," Myrin ordered me.

I obeyed, running to stand against it.

Venali looked ready to jump ship and swim to fight the enemy.

The pirates yelled and raised their weapons as they drew closer.

Didn't they realize something was wrong when we weren't fleeing or cowering?

They fired another cannonball, and Venali caught it in his hands. The pirates and I gaped. He pivoted, leaned back on one leg, and then threw the cannonball back at their ship. It hit their hull and crashed through it.

The pirates still drew closer, their greed outweighing their survival instincts.

Ryul looked at Myrin.

Myrin shook his head. "Let Venali have some fun."

Venali smiled wide and then roared at the pirates.

Daniel came up to his side, shifted, and roared as well.

"They've got a shapeshifter," one of the pirates yelled.

"Try to keep it alive, they sell well," another pirate yelled back.

Daniel snarled.

The ship drew alongside ours and both Venali and Daniel leapt aboard their ship, tearing through them with ease.

A couple pirates made it onto our ship, but Myrin dispatched them with a bored expression on his face, most of his attention on Venali and Daniel.

"Elara," Kydrus yelled.

I turned and immediately had to duck a pirate's sword.

Amrynn grabbed the pirate, snapped his neck, and tossed him into a small boat that had come up on the opposite side of the ship.

It had snuck over while we had been distracted.

Amrynn jumped down, killed all of the humans in the small boat, and then punched a hole in the bottom of it. He leapt back up onto our ship.

The boat and bodies sank.

I reached my hand out, and Amrynn took it, threading our fingers together.

Kydrus came to my other side and kissed my cheek.

I smiled up at him. "Thanks for the warning."

"You're always getting into trouble," he said with a shake of his head.

I stuck my tongue out at him and then faced the pirate ship again.

The screams had tapered down and there wasn't as much movement.

"All clear," Venali called.

Durlan stumbled up the stairs, rubbing his eyes. "Everything handled?"

"Yes, go back to sleep," Kydrus said.

Durlan yawned and stretched his arms up over his head, his shirt riding up enough to give me a view of the v of muscles below his belly button. He caught me looking and winked.

"I'm going to go over," Kydrus said. "Keep an eye on her, she almost lost her head," he said to Durlan.

Durlan looked down at me with a scowl. "Explain."

"Pirates," I said with a shrug, like that answered everything.

Durlan looked at Amrynn, a brow arched.

"A pirate snuck onto the ship while Venali and Daniel were on the other ship. We were all distracted by that chaos. She almost lost her head," Amrynn summarized.

"I ducked," I whispered.

A long sigh came from Durlan, but no words.

Venali hopped back onto our ship, a huge smile on his face.

"Have fun?" I asked.

He pulled me from Amrynn and kissed me deeply, his tongue sweeping across mine twice before he pulled back. "I did."

Daniel leapt onto our ship, now in his human form. Unlike Venali, he wasn't smiling.

I wanted to ask him what was wrong, but the stab of pain in my chest had me turning away instead.

"Anything good on their ship?" Amrynn asked.

"Yeah. Kydrus and Myrin are figuring out what to grab," Daniel said.

"I'll go help," Amrynn said. He slid his hand along my lower back as he passed, the warmth radiating up my spine.

"I'm going to practice," I said, pulling away from Venali.

"You think that's wise?" Daniel asked.

"It will give you time with Amara," I snapped. "So, why are you complaining? Or do you not want to talk to her either?"

He growled and stalked closer to me, but stopped when I looked up at him with tears in my eyes.

Venali set his hand on my hip, but I refused to look at him.

Instead, I let Amara out.

This time was different, though.

Normally, she took over, but this time it was more of a merger. I was still in control, but she could move us or use her powers.

"We've merged more," our combined voices said.

Venali and Durlan's eyes widened.

"We're going to have to stop this until I'm needed. If we merge much more, we won't be able to separate."

"Is that a bad thing?" Venali asked.

"It could be," we said.

"Because your plans to sacrifice yourself won't be possible?" Venali asked, his brows pinched.

"Yes."

"We don't want you sacrificing yourself," Daniel said.

"You don't get a choice," I said.

Daniel growled. "Why not just separate now? Let Elara go back to her life and we will continue with our mission."

Amara's power flared, and I lost consciousness.

CHAPTER 11
VENALI

THE CHANGEOVER WAS OBVIOUS. When Amara took over, her body glowed, her eyes glowed, and her aura changed.

"Why have you suddenly decided you dislike her?" Amara asked. "You didn't seem to have an issue the first day, when you sealed your mate bond."

He flinched. "That was before I realized she wasn't my true mate. You are, but you aren't her all the time."

"She is your true mate. Even if I was gone, you two would be bonded," Amara said.

Daniel scowled at her. "What?"

"It's complicated, I know, but she would have been your mate even if I hadn't chosen her," she said.

I shook my head. "That can't be right. The only reason Myrin and Daniel became her mate was because of your connection to her."

Amara laughed. "You boys are so dense sometimes. No, she's been bound to you since birth. My joining with her was part of it, but even if I separated from her now, you'd be hers still."

"That can't be," Myrin said, having returned to the ship. "I've always had my memories and the only time I sensed her was when your powers were awoken."

"Is this why you two have been so standoffish to her? This is why you've been making her cry?" Amara asked, her brows creasing and power flaring.

Myrin's eyes widened. "Cry?"

"Listen to me," she snarled. "If you hadn't merged with your hosts, they would be her mates. You are my mates, but you are also hers."

"Our bodies may be hers," Daniel said. "However, our souls are yours."

"And since I can't separate you from your bodies, what does that mean?" she asked, hands on her hips and a brow arched.

"That we're hers, too," Myrin said.

"Separate from her so we can end this," Daniel said.

"Why are you so bent on not falling for her?" Amara asked. "What will you do if we merge?"

"If you merge, it won't be a problem," Daniel said. "Right now, she isn't you most of the time. Now, this body may want her, but my soul..." He hit his chest. "My soul wants you. How can you make us endure this?"

She growled and marched up to him, stopping when she stood before him and then her feet floated above the deck until she was eye level to Daniel. "Endure? What are you enduring? A girl loving you? A girl wanting to touch you and speak to you? You endure nothing, but your own stupidity and stubbornness. She is the one enduring. She is the one planning to kill herself so she won't live without you. She is the one practicing day and night to fight a battle I've forced her to have a part in. You know nothing of her pain and sorrow. All you do is feel sorry that your body enjoys her and are blinded to what the truth is. She would sacrifice everything for you and you are acting like a...a..."

"Moron?" I suggested.

"Yes! A moron. Pull your head out of your furry butt before she dies and all you have left are regrets."

"Help us stop her from killing herself," Amrynn pleaded.

"No," Amara snapped. "She and I have our plans. She and I will figure this out. I'm half tempted to send you all away so you won't be such a distraction."

"Don't," I pleaded. "Daniel may have his doubts, but I was Elara's mate before my memories came back. I can't lose her."

"You're the one who won't talk to us and let us help you," Daniel snapped.

She spun back to face him, fury etched across her features. "The next time I see you will be when we've reached the shores of Zenlop. Try not to upset your mate between now and then."

"You're our mate," Daniel growled.

Light burst from her, making all of us shield our eyes.

"So is she. The sooner you accept that, the better. I mean it, if you cause her undue stress, she and I will leave you behind."

With that, her light faded, and Elara's body settled on the deck, her eyes closed.

After several tense moments of staring at her, Daniel stalked off.

There wasn't much we could say to him at this point.

Either he accepted what Amara had said, or we risked them fighting on their own.

I wouldn't let that happen.

Squatting down, I scooped Elara up in my arms and carried her to our room. Once she was tucked in, I returned to help transfer the items we'd found to our ship.

Myrin set the pirate ship on fire and Kydrus steered us clear of it.

No one spoke. All of us were absorbing Amara's words.

Whatever I had to do to keep Elara safe, I would do it. Even if it meant abandoning my brothers.

CHAPTER 12

ELARA

My body felt abnormally heavy, as did my soul. Instead of going up to the top deck, I stayed in bed, staring at the wooden beams overhead for several days.

I had no idea what Amara had told the guys, but they were more affectionate while seeming distant at the same time.

All of them, but Daniel.

He'd been missing for two days.

No, not missing...hiding.

I'd tried not to let it bother me, to be numb to the fact he suddenly didn't view me as a mate.

None of it worked.

Lying in bed, I tried again to numb myself.

It didn't matter because I likely wouldn't survive this battle anyway.

Footsteps approached.

I rolled over, facing away from the entryway.

"Are you going to lay in bed all day?" Amrynn asked.

"Yes," I replied.

He flopped onto the bed beside me, moving down so he could look into my eyes. "You need some sun. You're getting pale."

"I'm fine," I said. I used my power to draw on the sun, to fill my body with its warmth a moment and then released it. "There, I've had some sun."

He scowled. "Elara—"

"How close are we to our destination?" I asked.

"A day or two we think," he said.

I rolled over and closed my eyes. "Wake me then."

He left the room after placing a gentle kiss to my temple.

The day continued like that, with each guy stopping by trying to convince me to get up. Some brought me food, but none pushed me too hard.

At night, they took their shifts sharing the bed with me and on watch, but aside from soft words of love, they stopped trying to convince me.

The next two days, they didn't even try to ask me to leave. They'd sit with me a bit, bring me food and water, and that was it.

Finally, we reached Zenlop's shores.

I scarfed down a huge meal and then hurried to the figurehead.

There were long cannons atop walls lining the shores.

"I'll handle it," Amara said in my mind. "Tell the boys to shield their eyes."

"Shield your eyes," I yelled back to them.

Amara took control, but kept me conscious. She used my power of the moon to control the waves, creating larger and larger ones that had people running about. Then, a massive flare from the sun blinded everyone. She had the ship dock in the center of the docks and leapt into the middle of the people who were all covering their eyes.

Ryul placed a spell on the ship and then on us so we all appeared human.

Running, we moved as far into the town as we could before the humans could see again.

Amara's powers left, but I was still able to move with no issues. All of our practice had finally paid off.

Venali stayed at my side while the rest fanned out. We had decided a large group would draw too much attention.

The museum came into view, a small line waiting at the door, passing through machines that beeped.

"Metal detectors," I whispered.

Venali cursed. "I'll pass my sword to Myrin."

I nodded and continued forward, getting into line.

Once inside, I moved to the right to wait for Venali.

Ryul joined me instead. "He's checking the perimeter. Plus, I need to be in here to set my illusion."

We made our way around the exhibits, searching for the jar. I wasn't exactly certain what it looked like, but knew I would sense it.

When I was about to give up, I spotted it. The last item, near the exit.

Ryul and I stepped up to the glass box it sat in, both smiling.

"I never thought I would get this chance," Barry whispered in my ear.

Turning, I gaped at the gun now pressed to my side.

"When I was freed from the prison you put us in, I agreed to do whatever the man asked of me. Foiling your plot against him, getting a chance to kill you, those were bonuses."

Ryul growled, but I held up my hand.

"That man will destroy the universe. All he cares about is power," I whispered.

"He can destroy everything as long as you die," Barry hissed.

Ryul raised his hand, spinning his magic around the humans, and I spun away from Barry.

Barry smiled and shot me in the stomach. "Your illusions don't work on me."

I cried out and clutched at the pain and tried to stop the blood that flowed over my fingers.

Ryul kicked Barry's gun from his hand and then tossed him across the room.

Mustering my strength, pulling some from the sun, I shattered the glass box around the jar, grabbed it, and limped towards the exit.

Ryul picked me up and raced outside.

Alarms blared behind us and people in uniforms with weapons rushed after us.

Durlan, Myrin, Venali, and Kydrus teleported to us, and then teleported us to the ship.

I drew on my magic, pulled on the moon and had a huge wave of water pull us out into the sea.

The cannons exploded from the shores and cannonballs dropped around us.

Ryul set me down, and I cried out in pain.

"What happened?" Amrynn asked.

"Get us out," I snapped. "Now."

His eyes widened, and he rushed to the helm, steering us away.

Maniacal laughter floated on the wind. I knew it was Barry's.

Durlan tore my shirt open and started to heal me.

"There's a metal ball inside," I cried. I realized I was still holding the jar. "Myrin."

He stepped forward.

"Jar," I said, my lip trembling and body growing cold.

He took it and disappeared.

Daniel leaned down.

I wanted to swat him away, but had no strength.

"She's poisoned," he snarled.

Durlan pulled out a knife and pressed on my stomach, around my wound.

I screamed and felt like throwing up and passing out at the same time.

The cannonballs were still firing, but I couldn't tell how close. Sounds were distorted with some far away noises louder and close ones sounding far away.

"Ryul, charm her," Durlan said.

I whimpered.

Ryul set his hand on my head. "Dream happy dreams while Durlan fixes you up."

The ship disappeared, and I stood in the castle with Ryul. He tapped my arm and ran down the hallway.

"You're it," he yelled over his shoulder.

I laughed and ran after him.

CHAPTER 13

DANIEL

REGRET TUGGED at my heart and made my inner animal angry.

I knew I should have gone with them.

Instead, I had stayed on the ship, hiding below deck like I had been for a week.

Now, she was dying and there was nothing I could do to stop it.

I stood in the entryway to the room Myrin had built for her and stared at the small woman lying in the center of the bed.

My mate.

It had taken me several days to accept Amara's explanation.

As I stood there, I could feel our bond, proving Amara's point.

The bond thrummed, but much weaker than before.

Whatever the poison was that the bastard had used, it wreaked havoc on her system.

Even Durlan's powers couldn't defeat it. He had done his

best and the others took turns as well, but it seemed we had to let her body do the rest.

Elara whimpered in her sleep and sweat dotted her brow.

Without thought, I crossed the gap and sat beside her. Resting my hand against her head, I found it burning hot.

She stopped whimpering and pressed her face into my hand a bit.

Reaching over, I dipped the washcloth on the side table in water, and then draped it across her forehead.

She exhaled and her breathing evened out.

"I'm sorry," I whispered, spooning my body around hers. "Don't die on me, Elara. We need you. I need you."

She didn't respond.

"She'll pull through," Kydrus said from behind me.

I rolled over and stood. "How can you be so sure?"

He smiled as he looked at her, pure love glowing in his eyes. "Elara's always been a fighter. She's gone up against worse odds and pulled through."

"I wish I had known her before," I whispered. "You all have such a fondness for her it makes me wish I had known her longer."

"She's still very close to the same. Well, the same once she remembered a time before she was a slave," Kydrus said.

"You've known her the longest, right? Elara, I mean, not Amara."

He smirked. "I know who you meant. And, yes."

"Has she always been so..." I struggled for the right word.

"Frustrating? Endearing? Magnetic? Prone to danger? Yes," he said.

I chuckled.

"She wants to prove herself. She wants to save everyone.

She rushes in without a plan. She does all this and it all comes from her heart. She's one of the most pure and honest beings I have ever met. She wears her heart on her sleeve and it often got her into trouble. She's tried to close her heart, but she loves fiercely, so it is impossible for her to be alone. She lived alone while in Linta, where I ruled, and I could see the toll it took on her. I tried to get close to her, but fear ruled her then."

"It seems to rule her still," I said.

He nodded. "Fear of being alone and losing us definitely make up most of her decisions."

"I didn't believe Amara," I whispered. "I did just like Elara did with you; I tried to push her away. But I can't. She's part of me."

Kydrus set his hand on my shoulder. "She'll live through this. You'll get your chance to apologize."

Would she accept it, though?

He squeezed my shoulder and left.

I hoped he was right. I needed a chance to apologize, to beg her for another chance. To worship her as I would Amara.

CHAPTER 14

AMRYNN

IF I COULD, I would go right back to Zenlop, find Barry, and tear his head off.

That bastard had not only shot Elara, but had poisoned her as well.

My rage had no outlet, which only let it fester.

No matter how much we used our healing magic, we couldn't heal Elara.

Durlan sat beside me in the dining area, his shoulders slumped.

Perhaps I should have tried to console him, but no words came to mind.

Someone set a hand on my shoulder.

I grabbed their arm and jerked them forward, slamming their face against the table, my teeth bared and ready to tear out their throat.

Kydrus looked up at me with sad eyes. "Didn't mean to startle you," he said softly.

Quickly, I released him and sat back down.

"Any change?" Durlan asked.

Kydrus shook his head and sat beside me.

Durlan sighed, his eyes shadowed in darkness.

"Let's stop at the nearest port and see if we can find any medicines," Kydrus said.

Something I'd heard while captured on Barry's spaceship surfaced.

"What about a transfusion?" I asked Durlan.

He looked up at me. "Huh?"

"A blood transfusion. If we can cycle our blood into hers, maybe our magic will help her body fight the poison faster," I said.

Durlan's eyes widened, and he leapt to his feet. "Yes! Why hadn't I thought of that?"

"Do we have the items necessary for that procedure?" Kydrus asked.

"No, but if we can drop anchor, I can teleport to Emortalia, get the supplies, and teleport back," Durlan said.

It was difficult to teleport back to a ship, since it wasn't a stationary place.

"Are you sure?" I asked.

He smiled. "Worse that will happen is I teleport to the wrong place and have to swim a bit."

"We'll need to get near an island or somewhere with shallower water first," Kydrus said.

I stood and headed for the stairs. "I'll tell Myrin about our idea."

Finally, a chance to do something. A chance to help Elara.

The three of us raced to the helm, excited to tell Myrin.

We all came to a halt when a dark figure coalesced against the mast.

"I hear your pet is dying," a deep voice said from the figure.

"Leave," Myrin growled.

The figure looked at Myrin, his eyeless face still managing a glare somehow. "If it weren't for you, she would have been mine thousands of years ago."

Myrin smirked. "What can I say? I'm just more handsome than you."

The figure, the dark god, sped towards Myrin, but stopped just before him. "I'm here to offer you assistance. You would be wise not to anger me."

"We don't want your help," I snapped. "You helped enough by letting that maniac free."

"Give me the jar, and I'll give you the antidote. Your pet won't have to die," he said.

"No," all seven of us said at the same time.

"You're going to let her die?" he asked. "You're going to sacrifice that poor, innocent girl? For what? A plan that won't work?"

If it wouldn't work, he wouldn't try to get the jar from us. Plus, Elara almost died to get it. We couldn't give it up and let her pain be for nothing.

"How do we know your antidote would even work?" Myrin asked. "You could be poisoning her more instead of giving us an antidote."

"I may be ruthless at times, but I'm not heartless," the dark god said. He sighed, seeing we weren't swayed. With a flick of his wrist, he produced Elara's crown. "A show of good faith." He set it on the deck. "I'll be back tomorrow. You'll be a bit more willing to negotiate then, I'm sure."

He disappeared, and I raced to Elara. His statement had

fear coursing through my veins. No, she couldn't get worse. Not when we had a plan.

Elara's body was drenched in sweat, her cheeks red, and her breath came in pained gasps.

I tore the blankets from the bed, my eyes widening when I saw the blood staining the bandage over her gunshot wound.

"Durlan," I yelled.

"Already here," he said, cutting open her bandage.

Hovering on the far side of the room, I waited for his prognosis.

Please let her be okay. Please.

With quick efficiency, he changed out the bandage and then dabbed the wet washcloth from the side table against her face and neck.

"The poison's spreading," he whispered.

I hurried out to Myrin, who was speaking to Kydrus.

Everyone looked at me. "Her wound was bleeding again. Durlan said the poison is spreading."

Myrin altered our course.

"Maybe we should give him the jar," Ryul whispered.

"No," Daniel said. "That's exactly what he wants."

Ryul stood and stepped into Daniel's face. "Just because you don't care about Elara, doesn't mean she should die. Some of us love her, Amara or not."

Daniel shoved Ryul back. "You have no idea what I think."

"Let's find out," Ryul yelled and waved his hand.

Daniel's body tensed.

"Ryul, stop," Myrin snapped.

Ryul kept his eyes glued to Daniel, working his illusion.

As wrong as it was, I wanted to know how he felt about Elara, too.

Daniel growled and tried to move, but Ryul's magic held him in place. Tears dripped down his face, and he fell to his knees. He dropped his head into his hands and his body shook with sobs.

Ryul stepped back and nodded. "Fine, you can live, but remember that I could do this to you a million different ways all day for thousands of years. You hurt her again and what you just saw will be a dream."

Daniel looked up at us and then around as if searching for something with wide eyes. "What?" he rasped.

Ryul went below deck, a smart move considering Daniel's fury.

"What was that?" Daniel demanded.

"Ryul can make you see whatever he wants you to," Venali said. "I'm guessing he showed you Elara die?"

"She's...she's not..." Daniel looked around.

"No, she's alive," Myrin said. "He wanted to see if you actually cared about her."

"What did you see?" I asked.

"Durlan carried her dead body to us," Daniel said. He stood and headed towards the stairs, no doubt going to check on her.

Once he was gone, I looked up at Myrin. "Well, now we know he cares for her."

Myrin shook his head. "Ryul's going to get his ass kicked one of these days."

"Most likely," I agreed.

"How far to the nearest island?" Kydrus asked.

"Half a day," Myrin said.

"That far?" I asked and looked back the way Daniel had gone.

Would she survive that long?

"We need to keep the jar safe," Kydrus said. "He's clearly threatened by it."

Myrin nodded. "Let's rotate someone staying in the room with both Elara and the jar."

"What are we going to do when he comes back tomorrow?" I asked. "He could sink the ship or send more creatures after us."

Myrin tied the wheel to keep it headed in the correct direction and then dropped to his back on the deck with a dramatic sigh. "I don't know. I don't have all the answers."

Kydrus walked over and sat next to him. "You mean you aren't perfect?"

Myrin laughed. "Hardly. Part of me wants to give him the jar just so we can be sure Elara is safe. But I know she and Amara would be pissed and if they risked themselves like this, it's vital to their plan."

"The plan to sacrifice themselves?" I asked.

Myrin scowled. "Why couldn't Amara have found a vessel less stubborn than Elara?"

"Wouldn't have been hard," I muttered.

All three of us laughed.

"Food," Venali called from below deck.

"I'll bring you a plate," Kydrus told Myrin. "You just keep stewing on the ground."

"Thanks," Myrin said.

I waited until Kydrus left to approach Myrin.

He arched a brow at me.

"Barry being lose provides many possible issues," I said.

"Those humans were already more advanced than us if they had metal detectors. He could teach them how to make worse weapons and how to find Minloa."

He groaned. "Wonderful. We so needed a battle with the humans on top of everything else."

"A battle might help unite the Seelie and Unseelie," I said. "Especially if they see you fighting with us at Elara's side."

"Only if we survive this," he grumbled.

Only if Elara survived this.

"Any idea how to convince them to merge fully?" he asked me.

I laughed. "If I knew that, I would have done it already."

Myrin sighed. "Anxiety wasn't something I experienced before, but I find myself dealing with it daily now. How do we keep them both alive?"

"First, we get to an island so Durlan can get the items necessary for the transfusion," I said. "Then, we pray."

"It bothers me that Amara hasn't healed her. Is that a bad sign, or is it just not something she can do for her vessel?" Myrin asked.

"I've been wondering the same thing," I admitted.

CHAPTER 15

DANIEL

HER BODY BURNED with a fever that worried me more than the poison. High fevers in humans could cause brain damage. But she was Seelie, did that make a difference?

With gentle strokes, I dried the sweat from her body with a towel and then used the wet washcloth from the basin to try to cool her.

Ryul's powers had shown me her death, and it proved to me even more that I couldn't let her die. Seeing her dead body had shattered what was left of the wall I had built between us.

"You can fight this," I whispered in her ear. "You fought Cu Sith and redcaps. A poison should be child's play to you."

Carefully, I set her crown on her head, setting it so it rested on her hair.

The crown began to glow.

"Durlan," I yelled and stood from the bed, backing up in case some crazy magic started happening.

Durlan ran inside and his eyes widened. "What did you do?"

"I just set it on her," I whispered.

Elara's body began glowing and then she completely froze, no breathing and no heartbeat.

No. Had I just killed her?

We rushed forward, but Amara's voice whispered in our heads, "She's frozen herself. This will keep the poison from spreading and buy you some time. Leave her and hurry towards your healing solution."

My body shook as I stared at her seemingly lifeless body, but at least now I could sense the magic cocooning her.

"Stay with her," Durlan said. "Don't let the crown leave her head and keep the jar safe."

"Where are you going?" I asked and sat back on the bed.

"To see if we can make the ship move faster," he said. "I want to get the supplies as soon as possible so I can hear her heartbeat again."

We'd secured the jar by wrapping it in blankets and tied it to the wall so it couldn't fall and break. I double checked the blankets and then lay beside Elara.

"Hold on, beautiful. We'll save you soon," I whispered.

CHAPTER 16

KYDRUS

THE DARK GOD returned the next day, leaning against the mast in his shadowy black form again. "Your answer?" he asked.

"We will not give up the item we obtained. Be gone," Myrin growled.

The dark god sighed. "So be it."

He disappeared and then an ear-splitting roar made us all cover our ears.

The ship rocked and before the ship rose a sea serpent twice as big as any I had ever seen before.

"Wonderful," Venali said with a wide smile. "I've been itching to kill something." He cracked his knuckles and neck and walked towards the railing.

"Don't get reckless," Ryul called after him.

Venali rolled his eyes. "What are you, my mother?"

I snickered. "He'll be fine, Ryul. Let the big man have some fun and just sit back and enjoy the show."

Venali saluted me and faced the serpent. "Come on, you ugly, scaly, piece of carp!"

Apparently, the serpent understood our language because it screeched and tried to bite Venali.

Venali dodged its giant jaws, leapt up onto its head, and punched one of its eyes so hard that it exploded in a mess of goop and blood.

"Ouch," I whispered and cringed. I was all for killing the serpent, but that didn't mean I couldn't feel bad for it.

It thrashed and tried to dislodge Venali, but he held on to its now empty socket, laughing maniacally.

"He is definitely deranged," Ryul whispered.

Amrynn snorted.

Myrin threw a spear coated in his black flames into its throat. The flames spread quickly, but he kept them away from Venali.

Venali punched the serpent's head until the bone broke and then he fell into its skull.

"Uh..." I looked at Amrynn who was staring at the serpent and the spot Venali had fallen in with wide eyes as well.

Myrin extinguished his flames, likely unsure where Venali would come out and we all stood in silence as we waited to see what would happen.

"Should one of us—" Ryul's words were cut off by Venali roaring.

The serpent's head exploded, bits of it raining down on the boat and around us into the water.

Venali stood atop the ruined stump of the serpent, panting and snarling. Then, the serpent's body fell into the water with a loud splash and sent us careening backwards.

Venali teleported to us, flinging serpent goo off of him. "Well, that didn't go as planned."

I doubled over in laughter and everyone else joined in.

"Jump back in the ocean," Myrin ordered him. "You smell awful."

"Who wants sea snake steak for dinner?" Venali asked as he leapt overboard.

"Sounds great," I called down to him.

He scrubbed at his body in the sea water and then swam to the serpent and cut of some large chunks that he carried with him as he teleported back.

"You're all insane," Daniel said behind us.

We turned to find him standing at the steps, eyes wide and mouth agape.

We all just smiled at him, which earned us a headshake from him before he went back down to sit with Elara.

CHAPTER 17
ELARA

SOMETHING WARM WAS BEING PUMPED into my veins. It smelled like Venali.

Opening my eyes was a lot harder than it should have been.

What was going on?

Slowly, my eyes opened.

The room was dim, but I knew where we were instantly, the room in the ship.

"She's awake," Venali yelled.

I cringed. "Too loud."

"Sorry," he whispered and turned my head with his fingertips so he could look at me. He had tears in his eyes.

"Hi," I said softly.

Footsteps pounded on the wooden floor, and then all seven of my mates crowded into the room.

All were smiling.

"What's going on?" I asked.

Durlan rested his hand on my forehead and used his

magic to check me over. "It's gone," he whispered. "The poison is all gone."

"Poison?" I gasped. "What are you talking about?" I looked at the tube in my arm and fear consumed me. Memories of Barry using similar tubes to steal my blood flashed before my eyes. I tried to rip them out with a cry, but several pairs of hands held me down.

Durlan removed the tube and bandaged my arm where it had been.

Amrynn kissed my brow. "It's okay. It was necessary to heal you."

Durlan removed a similar tube from Venali's arm.

"Barry shot you with a bullet covered in poison," Amrynn said. "You've been unconscious for a week."

"A week?" I screeched.

"We are about a day out from Eltare," Myrin said.

"The jar?" I asked.

They all pointed to a bundle of blankets on the wall.

"Safe and secure," Ryul said.

"A week," I repeated.

"*He* tried to barter an antidote for the jar, but we refused," Daniel said. "He's sent dozens of creatures, but we've defeated them all."

I looked around at my guys and realized what I should have noticed sooner.

They were all exhausted.

Most had dark bags beneath their eyes and their normally straight backs were slumped. It took a lot to do this to Seelie warriors.

"You've been killing yourselves," I chastised. "You're all tired."

"We'll rest when we get to Eltare," Myrin said. He pushed his way to me and kissed my forehead. "I need to return to the helm. I'm glad you're doing better."

The rest took turns kissing me and heading out until it was just Daniel and I.

He cleared his throat while looking at the floor and shifted nervously.

I patted the bed. "Sit with me."

He sat and then pulled me into his arms. "I'm so sorry, Elara. I'm a jerk and I know I don't deserve your forgiveness, but I really am sorry. I care for you and part of me was worried that I was being disloyal to Amara, but—"

I set my hand over his mouth. "I forgive you."

He rested his forehead against mine and closed his eyes. "I'm an idiot. You're amazing and almost losing you really showed me how stupid I was."

"I'm still very immature," I whispered. "The situation could have been handled better on my end."

"Are you hungry?" he asked.

"Actually, I really need to pee," I said and stood on slightly wobbly legs. Luckily, they held and I was able to walk without assistance.

After using the restroom and grabbing a bunch of food, we went to the main deck so I could get some sun.

"You'd think sleeping for a week would mean I wasn't tired," I whispered as I leaned against Daniel and ate some soup.

He pet my hair. "Your body was doing all it could to keep you alive."

"Sea king," Myrin yelled.

I leapt to my feet just as an enormous sea snake surfaced.

It had spots on its body, teeth taller than me, and spikes along the side of its head.

Venali, Kydrus, and Amrynn were already on the move, racing forward across the deck with spears in their hands.

Daniel stepped in front of me. "Stay back, Elara. We've got this under control."

"You've fought one of these before?" I asked, still gaping at the huge creature.

"At least three," Daniel said.

"No wonder you all look so tired," I said softly. "You've been fighting a lot."

Daniel reached back and gripped my hand with his. "It's all worth it."

Two of the spears pierced the creature in its eyes, and the last went through its head.

It fell back into the water, causing a wave of water to push us away from it.

"That quickly?" I gasped.

"We've become efficient," Myrin said from the helm. "It helps save energy."

My mates, Amara's consorts, really were something special.

I had to do whatever I could to keep them alive.

Myrin tapped my forehead and bent to look into my eyes. "No."

"No, what?" I asked and rubbed my head even though it hadn't hurt.

"Whatever you're thinking. You've got your sad and serious face on. That usually means you're planning something stupid or dangerous. Or both," he said.

I leaned forward and kissed him. "I love you, Myrin."

He rested his hand on my cheek and rubbed his thumb across the bone. "I love you, too, Elara."

I pressed closer to him and slid my hands up his chest. "More than cookies?' I asked with a playful smirk.

He dropped his hand and stroked the side of my breast as he caressed my side, stopping at my hip. "More than cookies."

I tugged on his shirt. "Off."

He removed his shirt without question.

Taking my time, I memorized every inch of his exposed flesh. He was my Unseelie king.

With a jump, I wrapped my arms around his neck and my legs around his waist, and then kissed him.

He supported me easily, my weight meant nothing to him, and kissed me back.

Another set of hands slid around me from behind to cup my breasts.

I gasped into Myrin's mouth, but he just devoured the sound.

Myrin pried me off and set me on my feet.

Intending to object, I opened my mouth, but he pressed his hand over it.

Then, he tugged my shirt off and dropped to his knees to fondle and suck on each of my breasts.

Daniel, the one who had been behind me, spread my legs and rubbed me through my pants.

I arched my upper body forward into Myrin and my lower body backwards into Daniel.

Myrin stood, and I stuck my hand down his pants to grip his erection. He groaned and dropped his head back.

Daniel jerked my pants down, spread my legs even wider, and inserted himself into my wet core. He moved in and out slowly, letting my body adjust to him. Once fully inserted, he began pumping his hips.

I pumped my hand on Myrin at the same pace, watching his face to gauge his pleasure.

Daniel withdrew and spun me around.

Myrin slid into me, gripping my hips tightly.

I reached for Daniel, and as I slid my hand along his slick erection, he rubbed my aching nub.

The three of us developed a rhythm and it wasn't long before I screamed my first orgasm.

Myrin withdrew and spun me.

I expected to face Myrin, but faced Venali instead.

I reached up and traced my fingertips over his scar.

He dropped his pants, and I bent over, taking him in my mouth.

Hands gripped my butt and someone else entered me. I turned my head slightly.

Ryul.

He slammed into me hard and fast, making me orgasm three times before Venali finished in my mouth.

Someone grabbed my hair and pulled me into a standing position.

Durlan.

He took his time, building my orgasm, and then right when I was about to come, he pinched my nipple and pulled tighter on my hair.

The orgasm was the strongest yet. I screamed, and he didn't stop, pounding into me and squeezing my breasts.

He withdrew right before my next climax and before I could complain, Amrynn dropped to his knees and began licking and sucking my even more sensitive nub.

Kydrus slid into me while Amrynn continued licking me. Daniel and Myrin each took a breast and started sucking on them while rubbing themselves.

Kydrus withdrew and then inserted his fingers into me while he stroked himself. "Scream for us, beautiful."

My eyes rolled up into my head as all the stimulation caused an eruption from me. I cried out and so did the four guys with me.

When I opened my eyes, I found four spots of spilled seed on the deck.

My legs wobbled and Kydrus picked me up.

"Well, that was interesting," a deep voice said.

We turned, facing a dark shadowy figure.

The dark god.

"I see you survived," he said to me.

"I did. Thank you for returning my crown," I said with a smile.

His eyeless, smoky form smiled. "See, boys, this is how you're supposed to act."

"What do you want?" Myrin asked.

I realized none of them had bothered to get dressed, and they were all standing in their nude glory, staring at the dark god.

"Give me the jar," he said.

"You'll get it soon enough," I said, still smiling pleasantly at him.

"It won't work," he said.

I shrugged. "Only one way to find out."

"You test my patience," he snarled.

Amara took over, letting me stay again. "You test ours," we snapped. We flung our hand out, and his shadows exploded and then disappeared.

Amara left, and I slumped in Kydrus's arms.

"Stop doing that," Kydrus growled.

"Tell Amara, not me," I whispered and snuggled into him.

"Let's get dressed," Myrin said. "We're close to Eltare."

Eltare, the home of the Unseelie. It felt like a lifetime ago that we had been there.

By the time we'd gotten dressed and my hair was brushed, we were docked at Eltare.

I carried the jar in my arms, cradling it like a baby as we made our way to the castle.

Aerith met us out front and bowed to me. "Your Majesty," she said. "We are honored to have you back."

"Have preparations been made while I was away?" I asked and walked up the steps towards her.

She looked at Daniel with an arched brow, but wisely didn't comment on his presence. "Yes. Once you give the word, my people will be ready to go."

I nodded. "Good. We need two days to rest and then on the third day, we will leave at dawn. Let your people know."

Myrin opened the castle door for me, and we made our way to the room we'd used last time.

Venali checked the room and then opened the door for us all to enter.

Once inside with the door closed, the guys crawled onto the bed and promptly fell asleep.

I set the jar down, still wrapped in the blankets, and sat on the floor.

They were all exhausted, but I wasn't.

So, I took my first ever turn as lookout while they slept. My lookout turn was uneventful and boring.

When they all finally woke the next day, I'd created a mini universe with rocks that orbited each other like planets would.

They all stared at my tiny rocky universe in silent rapture.

I let the rocks fall to break their transfixion.

"I'm hungry," I said.

"How long did we sleep?" Durlan asked and ran a hand through his hair.

"A full day," I said and stood, groaning at my sore butt.

"Have you eaten?" Amrynn asked.

I shook my head. "I didn't open the door at all."

"You should have woken one of us," Daniel chastised me.

I shrugged. "You guys obviously needed the rest." Sticking my head out the door, I spotted a castle servant and waved him over.

He ran to me and bowed.

"Is it dinner time yet?" I asked.

"In an hour, Your Majesty," he said. "Would you like me to fetch you some food?"

"No, just let your queen know my mates and I will be coming for dinner," I instructed.

He bowed and ran off.

I waved down another castle servant, a female this time. "Can you escort us to the bathing area?"

She curtsied. "Certainly."

We followed her, and I admired her curly hair as it bounced about her shoulders.

I caught Kydrus watching her hair, too, and twirled my straight hair around my finger with a scowl.

Myrin looped an arm around my waist and squeezed. "Your hair is beautiful," he whispered in my ear. "No one has such unique coloring."

The bathing area was a huge cavern filled with dozens of pools of water, large enough for three people to fit in each one.

She handed each of us soap bars and pointed at a stack of towels. "I will ensure no one disturbs you while you bathe. Do you need your clothing washed?"

"Please," I said with a smile. I stripped from my clothes and handed them to her.

She took them with wide eyes and then quickly averted her gaze.

"Ours, too," Venali said.

All of the guys stripped and piled their clothes atop mine.

I wasn't sure her cheeks could get redder. She curtsied and hurried away, all but running.

The guys snickered and each climbed into separate pools, far apart from one another.

Scowling, I looked at them. Was I supposed to choose one? I didn't want to choose one.

Grumbling beneath my breath, I climbed into my own separate pool, close to the door. I moaned as the warm water slid around me like a comforting hug. Healing magic from the water seeped into me.

"Keep moaning like that and that girl will be even more embarrassed when she comes back and catches us in the act," Daniel said.

Floating in the pool, I closed my eyes and ignored him.

Something splashed in my pool, causing waves of water to splash over my face.

I spluttered as I sat up, then my jaw dropped.

Venali and Myrin held a male Unseelie by the arms, keeping him back as he tried to stab me.

The attacker growled at me and bared his teeth.

I stood, stepped into his face with my teeth bared, let a bit of power out, and growled back.

He stilled and then tried to back away, but Venali and Myrin held him too tightly.

"Who sent you?" I asked.

He shook his head and closed his eyes.

"Durlan," I called.

Durlan walked over and bowed to me. "Yes, my queen?"

"See if you can find anything from the knife," I said.

The attacker's eyes snapped open and he tried to thrash and escape, but he was no match for Venali.

Durlan touched the knife, and then growled loudly. "I know who sent him."

"Venali, knock him out. Dinner is about to get very interesting."

Venali's magic sparked and the man instantly slumped, eyes closed and breathing even.

They carried him out of my pool and tossed his body on the ground.

Durlan helped me out of my pool and into another one.

This time, I washed quickly instead of enjoying the water.

The girl returned with our clothes and gaped at the unconscious man. "How did he get in here?"

I waved at her dismissively. "Don't worry about it. Are our clothes clean?"

She nodded and sorted the piles.

I climbed out and she rushed me over a towel, keeping her eyes averted.

Except, the guys got out of their pools in her line of sight, so she had to avert her gaze to the ceiling, blushing again.

"It's okay," I whispered and took the towel.

"Would you like me to brush your hair?" she asked.

"No," Myrin said. "We'll take care of it. Just leave the brush."

She nodded, curtsied, and ran off, dropping the brush on a bench as she passed it.

"I wanted her help," I mumbled as I dried off.

Myrin dressed and picked up the brush. "I wanted to do it, though."

That was something I wouldn't say no to.

I sat and he sat behind me, taking my hair into his hands and began brushing the tangles out.

The others got dressed and then sat around me, watching.

It felt incredibly intimate, yet all that was happening was my hair being brushed.

When he finished brushing it, he helped me stand, and smiled. "Ready?"

I felt ready to take on the universe. "Yes," I said.

Venali picked up the unconscious man, and we exited the bathing area.

Clean and rested, we walked down the hallway with our heads held high.

Together, we could accomplish anything.

I just had to keep them together.

Guards gaped at Venali carrying an Unseelie, but opened the door to the dining hall without questions. Venali's glower likely had something to do with their silence.

The room was full of Unseelie, and as last time, Aerith sat at the head table.

Venali dropped the man on the table, splashing food everywhere.

Aerith's eyes widened. "What's the meaning of this?" she asked, anger and confusion on her face.

Oh, she was an excellent actress.

"That's what I want to know," I said. "Are you such a coward that you couldn't even attempt to kill me yourself?"

She bristled and stood. "I am no coward and I didn't—"

I held up my finger, stopping her. "Be very careful with your next words. I do not tolerate liars."

Unlike Seelie, Unseelie could lie.

She folded her arms across her chest. "What proof do you have that I was involved?"

I waved at Durlan.

He stepped forward, touched the dagger, and the scene of her paying the man to kill me was projected above us.

"That's fake," she snapped and walked around the table. "You're just trying to steal my throne."

"Your throne holds no interest to me," I said.

"Why do you have a human among your consorts?" she asked. "What kind of *Empress* debases herself with a human?"

"Shift," I ordered Daniel without turning to look at him.

He came to stand behind me, his warmth pressing against my back, and shifted into his bear form, towering over me. He roared and it echoed in the room.

Unseelie gasped, and a couple of women screamed.

"These men are more than meets the eye," I said.

"Apologize and we'll forget it happened," Myrin said.

"I did nothing," she growled and bared her teeth.

"Ryul," I called.

He lifted his hand and she instantly began screaming and fell to her knees.

I let her scream for a full minute and then lifted my hand.

Ryul dropped his hand and Aerith panted on the floor.

"Admit to your people what you did," I said.

"I tried to kill her," she whispered.

"Louder," Myrin roared at her.

"I tried to kill her," she yelled and wiped at her face. "Unseelie and Seelie shouldn't mix. The Seelie are pompous and arrogant. They won't accept us."

"I have Seelie, Unseelie, and shapeshifter mates," I said loud enough to be heard throughout the room. "Clearly, they can coexist. You're as blinded by your hatred as the old Seelie."

The crowd murmured.

"Who is next in line?" I asked Myrin.

"Besides me?" he mumbled.

I rolled my eyes. "Obviously." Then, scowling I said, "Unless you want to be king."

"Larissa is next," he said.

I turned and searched the crowd. "Larissa?"

The girl who'd taken us to the bathing chamber stood.

My eyes widened, and Myrin gave me a small nod of affirmation.

"I hereby remove Aerith as queen and thus power goes to Larissa as next in line."

"You can't," Aerith yelled and drew power.

All of my mates tensed, but I stepped forward and stared into Aerith's eyes with no fear. "Try me."

Her eyes widened, and she tried to strike me with a bolt of electricity.

I absorbed the electricity with a smile, let the sun fill me, and burned her to a pile of dust. Her crown was all that survived. "I am Empress of the Galaxy. I am Goddess of the Universe," I said. I turned and smiled at the shocked Unseelie. "Our peoples will unite and those who oppose me may challenge me or my mates. Anyone care to challenge us?"

No one moved. I wasn't even sure they were breathing.

Releasing my powers, I smiled. "Good. Now, let's eat."

A few servants cleared the body of my attacker, dust of the old queen, and spilled food.

Larissa sat on the throne, smiling.

I picked up the crown, blew off bits of Aerith dust, tried to shine it with my shirt, and held it out to Larissa. "It needs washing, but this is yours."

She bowed. "I hope to be a better ruler than our previous monarch."

I winked. "You'll do great."

When Myrin sat beside me, I leaned over and asked, "Why didn't her guards intervene?"

He leaned close enough for our shoulders to touch. "Venali kept smiling at them. I don't think they breathed the entire time."

Venali leaned across the table and whispered, "I was inviting them to intervene. It's not my fault they're cowards."

"Also, there was a massive bear standing behind you," Kydrus whispered.

Daniel snickered.

Kydrus made a plate for me and then Daniel took it and smelled it.

I arched a brow, and he set it down. "I'm not taking chances," he said with no shame.

The guys chatted, telling Daniel what to expect when we reached Minloa.

Discreetly glancing around, I expected fear to still be present on the Unseelie in attendance, but most were smiling.

It appeared that Aerith had been disliked by several people.

A couple dozen people approached Larissa, giving their congratulations and support.

Good.

I saw my old self in her and hoped that meant she'd help those most in need now that she was ruler.

CHAPTER 18
ELARA

LARISSA STOOD on the docks to see us off. A dozen Unseelie joined us for the trip, leaving behind their friends and families to become ambassadors in Minloa.

I waved and smiled to all of the Unseelie gathered on the docks.

"You look so queen-like," Venali whispered in my ear.

I chuckled and looked up at him. "Seems that I'm finally falling into my role, huh?"

He kissed my cheek. "You've always been a queen to me."

We set sail and I spent the time beating Ryul at dice.

The trip to Minloa was short, yet it felt like it took days. I had been gone for so long and I felt like a completely different person.

Myrin and Venali stayed with the Unseelie once we docked to help them get settled.

The rest of us teleported to the castle courtyard.

Guards rushed forward, but slowed when the recognized us.

One of the new warlords came forward and bowed. "Welcome back, Your Majesty."

I smiled. "Thank you." I would have added his name if I had remembered it.

"Any troubles while we were gone?" Durlan asked, stepping forward.

Amrynn stepped up next to me and whispered, "You don't remember his name, do you?"

"You guys picked and trained them," I mumbled. "How am I supposed to remember their names?"

"Your Majesty, are you aware there's a human with you?" one of the guards asked.

I sighed. "No, my consorts and I had no idea a giant human had hitched a ride."

The guard blushed.

"This is Daniel. He is one of my other consorts," I said. "Make sure all of the castle staff know."

"Yes, Your Majesty," he said and bowed.

"Oh, and you'll likely start seeing Unseelie around as well. Don't attack them or you'll pay," I added as I skipped into the castle.

I twirled around as I skipped down the hallway. Home. We were finally home.

CHAPTER 19

DANIEL

KNOWING Elara was a queen and seeing her in her castle were two different things.

As soon as she stepped foot inside, her entire body relaxed and she started humming.

Watching her twirl about, a smile on her face...it stole my breath.

Mine.

My mate.

I would do whatever I could to keep her alive. Her plan to sacrifice herself would not come to fruition.

"Stunning, isn't she?" Kydrus whispered to me.

I nodded.

"When she's here, another side of her comes out. I like to think this is the true Elara, the one she would be if Amara hadn't chosen her."

Unsure how to respond to that, I just watched Elara.

She spun in a circle, but her feet tangled, and she fell onto the hallway's carpet runner. She laughed and Ryul helped her up.

"You always trip on that spot of carpet," Ryul said and shook his head.

She chuckled. "Maybe I should replace that patch."

He laughed. "You'd still trip."

She linked her hand with his and continued skipping down the hallway, forcing Ryul to lengthen his stride to keep up.

"Skip with me," she said to him.

"I'm not a child anymore," he said.

"Apparently you're an old, boring geezer," she said as she pulled her hand away.

Ryul growled, but it was obviously playful. "Take that back."

She walked backwards so she could face him. "Old. Boring. Geezer," she said, punctuating each word.

Ryul dashed forward, but Elara spun and took off down the hallway with a high-pitched, girly shriek.

"They were childhood friends?" I asked.

"Yes," Amrynn said from my right. "He saved her from the planned assassination of her family. He froze her in a crystal and then he waited a thousand years, alone, in this castle, for her to return."

My respect for Ryul increased dramatically. Even before his memories, he had been loyal to Elara.

Elara ran back towards us, pushing between Amrynn and I, and then hid behind my back, peeking her head around my side.

Ryul raced towards us, hands out, ready to grab her. "You can't run forever," he said, grinning wider than I had ever seen him before, even our prior life.

He darted around Kydrus, but Elara ran around Amrynn,

in front of me. "Your joints will start hurting soon and you'll be ready for your nap, geezer."

"I'm older than he is," Amrynn said and folded his arms across his chest. "What's that make me?"

Elara's eyes sparkled. She backed away from us and yelled, "Ancient," before running away.

Kydrus and Amrynn exchanged a glance, and then both ran after her.

Ryul walked next to me as we followed, watching her dodge their half-hearted attempts to catch her.

"You okay?" Ryul asked.

I nodded, not taking my eyes off her. "Just wishing I'd been here sooner."

Ryul patted my shoulder. "Me too, brother. Me, too."

A tall Seelie man came out of a room with his head bowed over a book, stepping right into Elara's path.

She crashed into him, making him drop his book.

"We don't run in the hallways," he growled, bending to pick up the book.

Elara stood and folded her arms over her chest. "I'll do whatever I want."

He raised his eyes, power flaring, but the instant he saw her face, he dropped to a knee with his head bowed. "Forgive me, Your Majesty."

She patted his shoulder, her wide smile back in place. "No worries, I hate when I'm interrupted from reading, too."

Amrynn reached out to grab her and she started running again.

The man watched her go, eyes wide and mouth open.

"She's one of a kind," Ryul said to him as we passed.

"That she is," the man said softly.

When we finally caught up to her, Elara was sprawled on the carpet, panting.

"Food," she groaned. "So hungry."

Ryul picked her up and tossed her over his shoulder. "Come on, Your Majesty. I'll take you to get some food."

"And dessert?" she asked, raising her head.

"Only if you eat your vegetables," he said.

An ache formed in my chest. A combination of regret for the few days I had been a jerk to her, and remorse over not knowing her before she'd merged with Amara.

Everyone had pointed ears except for me and none could shift. Would I feel like an outsider while here?

Once in the kitchen, Elara sat on a counter and patted the spot next to her while smiling at me.

I hopped up beside her and watched as she kicked her legs back and forth.

So innocent and childlike, that was how she was acting.

"Durlan makes really good food," Elara said. "Venali is the best cook, but neither are here, so we will have to suffer through whatever those three can make."

"Elara," I whispered. My mouth closed, unsure what to say.

She looked up at me, smiling and so happy. "Yes?"

"I love you," I whispered.

She scooted closer until our hips and legs touched and said, "I love you, too, Daniel."

I draped my arm around her shoulders and hugged her against my side.

I would kill a thousand men, a universe of gods, or whatever I had to as long as it would keep that smile on her face.

CHAPTER 20

DURLAN

"You're certain it was him?" I asked Karlo, the new Warlord of Blustum.

He nodded. "I saw him myself. I used to live nearby, so I know what he looked like.

I snarled. We should have thought about the possibility of Feno returning once she opened Minloa to the Unseelie.

If he wanted to upset her and possibly further the discord between the Seelie and Unseelie, all he had to do was confront her in front of a crowd.

"Where and when did you see him?" I asked.

He pointed to Adlin, Menma's main city. "Here, near the river, four days ago."

Feno couldn't teleport, and Klinsot was a five day journey from Adlin by foot.

"Double patrols, but order them not to engage with Feno. You contact me immediately when you see him."

"Yes, sir," Karlo said.

The moment I saw Feno, I would tear his head off. He wouldn't lay a finger on Elara.

I followed the pull of our bond, winding my way through the castle to find her.

My searching lead me to the kitchen where I found Elara wrestling with Ryul, trying to grab a cookie he held out of her reach.

All of them were smiling and looked happy for the first time together.

Amrynn and Kydrus walked to me, their smiles gone.

"What's wrong?" Kydrus asked.

"Later," I said, my eyes back on Elara exaggeratedly pouting at Ryul who still had the cookie.

"Consort meeting tonight?" Amrynn asked.

I nodded and stepped around them. A smile lit up my face, and I snatched the cookie and held it out to Elara.

Her mouth opened as she smiled and took the offered cookie from my hand. Ryul stepped towards her and she shoved the whole cookie into her mouth, making her cheeks puff out.

We watched as she tried to chew it, but it was too large and she started choking.

Daniel handed her a glass of water, and I patted her back.

She sniffled, looking at the cookie pieces on the ground.

"If you'd eaten your vegetables, this wouldn't have happened," Ryul chided her.

"My cookie," she whispered. Raising her head, she had tears in her eyes. "That was the last one."

I wiped her eyes and smiled. Moments like this, moments when she could be carefree were my favorite. "I'll make you some more, okay?"

"Really?" she asked and wiped her nose.

What would her life have been like without Amara interfering?

I bent and kissed her. "Really, but you'll have to help."

She ran to the cupboards and started pulling out ingredients.

If necessary, I would hunt Feno down to keep Elara from having to deal with him and the painful memories he brought.

Ryul looked at me.

"Consort meeting tonight," I whispered.

His eyes widened and he nodded.

Rolling up my sleeves, I washed my hands and then smiled at Elara. "Let's make some cookies."

CHAPTER 21
VENALI

DURLAN HAD CALLED A CONSORT MEETING, and I'd had to use my magic to knock Elara out, so she wouldn't interrupt us.

I spun a pencil between my fingers, anxiety coursing through me. Durlan wouldn't have called the meeting unless it was something important.

Hopefully, it was something for me to kill.

Myrin sat beside me and sagged in his chair.

"Rough day?" I asked.

"I've had to answer five billion questions about what it's like being Unseelie. Why did your ancestors have to be such dicks?"

I chuckled. "It'll get better."

"It's about to get a lot worse," Durlan said as he slammed the door closed. Then, he put a seal on the door so no sound would escape.

I leaned forward, smiling. "I get to kill something?"

Durlan looked at me and the fire and anger I saw startled me. "He needs killing, and while I'd prefer to do it, I don't care which of us ultimately snuffs his life out, as long as he fucking dies."

All of us gaped at him. He never cursed.

"Who?" I asked, gripping my pencil.

"Feno," Durlan said.

I snapped my pencil in my hand and stood. "Where was he last seen?"

"Sit," Durlan snapped.

I growled, but complied. That bastard was still alive? Durlan was right, he needed to die. And soon. Before he got near Elara.

Glancing at Ryul, I realized he wasn't shocked. "You knew?" I asked.

"I assumed," Ryul said.

"There's more," Durlan said, getting our attention. "Fae creature attacks have tripled the past month."

"Too many for the Warlords to handle?" I asked.

Durlan nodded. "And they're seemingly random."

He set markers on several spots around Minloa. My eyes widened as he continued setting them, putting over a dozen down.

"This is just last week," he said.

"Where are they coming from?" Kydrus asked. "We never had that high of a population before."

"That's my question," Durlan said. "I think we need to search out where they're coming from."

"It would make sense that *he* is sending them," Ryul said. "Trying to separate us from her."

He had a point.

"I don't think separating is a good idea," Daniel said.

"Leaving her without all of us would be the perfect time for *him* to attack."

"We can't just let our people die," Durlan growled.

"Easy," I said sternly to Durlan.

His head whipped towards me and he bared his teeth at me. Several tense moments later, he dropped his head and took a large breath which he exhaled audibly. "Sorry."

"Why don't we take Elara around the realms?" Amrynn asked. "She could see her people, greet them, and be seen to make the people accept her more. And, we could do some investigation at the same time."

"Two birds, one stone," I said, smiling.

Myrin nodded. "It's a good idea."

"And it will give the people time to see and get used to you two," Kydrus said and looked at Myrin and Daniel.

Durlan sat down and nodded. "I like it, but it does put her at more risk for attacks."

"We can't hide her in the castle," Ryul said. "The people will hate her if she doesn't walk among them."

"What about a ball?" I asked.

All eyes focused on me, most wide.

"You want to hold a ball?" Kydrus asked.

"A ball always makes the people happy," I added.

"Why not both? She could announce the ball to everyone she visits," Kydrus said.

"A personal invitation from the queen," Durlan said and smiled. "Yes, that's perfect."

"If we don't kill Feno before the ball, you know he will show up and try to kill her," I growled.

"It's too good an opportunity for her to solidify her place

here. We should also invite the Unseelie, so they can mingle," Myrin said.

Elara burst into the room, shattering the door and breaking Durlan's spell. Her eyes glowed, not with Amara's power, but her own. "You spelled me," she snapped. "To have a secret meeting. What have you decided without me this time? What about my future have you planned for me?"

Her power made a wind swirl around her, and I realized her feet weren't even touching the ground.

"We're going to host a ball," I said. "So the Seelie and Unseelie can meet."

"And we thought it would be a nice gesture if you visited each Realm and gave the invitation to your people yourself," Kydrus added.

In an instant, her power was gone, and she stood before us with disheveled hair and sleep rumpled clothes. "Oh." She looked at the markers and her brows furrowed. "What else?"

I started to stand, but she pointed at me, so I froze.

"You do not get to approach me right now. I'm still pissed you used that damn spell on me again," she said and growled at me.

I smiled at the most perfect and glorious woman in existence, and took my seat again.

She pointed. "Explain."

"The number of fae creature attacks have increased," Durlan said. "We're unsure where they're coming from."

She walked around the table, keeping as far from me as possible, and then froze and her face lost all color.

Daniel started to reach out for her, but she raised a shaking hand and pointed at the markers. "It's him," she whispered. "It's a message."

We all crowded to her side and looked at it. Knowing it was a word, or words, made seeing it easier.

Soon.

He'd orchestrated attacks so that the markers on the map would spell the word, soon.

Elara wrapped her arms around herself, but we could all see her shaking and sense her fear.

Myrin picked her up and whispered into her ear too low for me to hear.

She nodded, and he carried her out of the room.

We continued staring at the word and anger built within me until I was ready to burst.

I swiped the markers off the table. "I can't wait to kill that bastard."

CHAPTER 22

ELARA

For a full day, I lay in my room, staring at the jar.

He had done it to upset me. So, I shouldn't have let it upset me. However, that was much easier said than done.

"Elara," Daniel whispered as he sat beside me.

"When I die, who is going to take over ruling Minloa?" I asked. "I need to find and appoint an heir, since I won't have one of my own."

"Why won't you have one of your own? And you aren't going to die."

"Daniel, everyone dies," I said.

"Why won't you have one?" he asked again.

"I refuse to get pregnant. If I die during this battle, I don't want it to be while I'm carrying a child," I said.

"Let me guess," he said. "You and Amara worked out a deal?"

"Sort of," I said. "She made me infertile for the time being."

He growled.

"Growl all you want; I'm not changing it."

"Why are you so certain you're going to die?" he asked softly. "There has to be a way for us all to live."

"If we all live, that means you'll leave me to be with Amara," I whispered.

He tensed and said nothing.

"I don't want to live without you," I whispered back. "And I don't want to make you choose. You are Amara's mates first. You were separated for so long and you deserve to be together. I won't stand in the way of that."

"So, you're going to kill yourself?" he asked.

"No, I'm going to ensure you all survive," I said. "Hopefully, this jar will contain him. Then, Amara and I can decide what to do from there."

I wouldn't tell him our main plan because he and the others would try to stop us.

"You need to eat. Come on," he said and picked me up.

I snuggled against his chest and kissed the side of his neck. I would miss him so much if I had to live without him. It hurt thinking about it.

"Can't I wear pants?" I asked and tugged at the green dress I wore.

The guys had insisted I wear a dress and my crown to visit my people. Personally, I was certain they did it just to mess with me.

"You're a queen and queens shouldn't whine," Durlan said and brushed my hair over one shoulder.

"Do goddesses whine?" I asked.

Ryul snickered and then clamped his lips shut.

"Do you have the invitations?" Kydrus asked.

I held up the basket with a dozen rolled up invitations. "Here."

"Are we missing anything?" Amrynn asked.

Myrin phased through the wall next to me. "Me," he said.

I squealed and then smacked his arm. "You did that on purpose. The door is open."

His wide smile didn't falter.

"Okay, let's go," Durlan said.

"Where to first?" I asked.

"Crol," Amrynn said with a wide smile and set his hand on my shoulder.

We teleported right into the town square, atop a platform that had not been there last time I had visited.

Amrynn stepped back and I realized the courtyard was filled with Seelie, who looked at me expectantly, which meant they'd been warned of my arrival.

I cleared my throat and took one of the invitations from the basket and then gave the basket to Kydrus.

"People of Blustum, I've come today to extend an invitation," I said.

Several people whispered to each other.

"Amrynn," I called and then handed him the invitation to nail to the well in the middle of the courtyard.

As he did so, I continued, "I am hosting a ball, to celebrate my return and the unification of alliances I have made."

"Did you make the alliances by taking a man off their hands?" someone asked and snickered.

"Since when do queens associate with humans?" another asked.

I sighed. "Why are you all so ridiculous? Look." I waved at Daniel, who shifted into a bear. "He's not human. Secondly, it is none of your business who I take as a consort."

"Until she takes all the men, and we've got none left," a woman jeered.

"Jealousy is an ugly thing, Trinity," Amrynn said. "Since when do the people of Blustum lack respect and honor?"

"Who lacks honor?" a man shouted from the back of the crowd.

Amrynn waved his hand at everyone in the crowd. "All of you. Instead of insulting our queen and her consorts, why don't you challenge us to a duel?"

No one spoke.

"Lack of honor," Amrynn said and shook his head.

"I came here to invite you to a ball, to personally invite you. I only have one goal, to unite us. We've been segregated for too long. I hope you will come, but this is not mandatory. I would never try to force this. I realize you don't know me. I came to get to know you better, but if I am not wanted here, I will move on to another realm."

"Wait," a little girl cried out.

I squinted my eyes as I tried to find her, and finally spotted her trying to squeeze through the adults.

I jumped down from the platform, almost face planting because of the dress, and faced the Seelie before me. "Let her pass," I ordered them, but in a nice tone.

Many moved out of her way, but several still blocked her.

Kydrus jumped down next to me, raised his hands and acted like he was pushing something apart.

The people before me parted, creating a lane for the girl.

Most of the people Kydrus had moved gaped with open mouths.

I turned and kissed his cheek. "Thanks."

The little girl stopped before me, panting.

I knelt, not caring that my dress was getting dirty, and smiled at her. "What's your name?"

"Cassie," she said. She took a deep breath, her cheeks red, and said, "I'd like you to have this." She held out a beautiful purple flower.

I gently took it. "This is beautiful. I've never seen this type of flower before."

"I crossbred my favorite flowers to make it," she said.

Carefully, I tucked the flower above my ear. "Does it look okay?" I asked her.

She smiled wide and nodded quickly.

"Thank you, Cassie. I hope you'll come to my ball," I said.

"I'll try," she said and looked behind her, I presumed towards her parents.

I stood and she tugged on my dress to get my attention again.

I looked back down.

"Can...can I meet the other warlords, er, your consorts?" she asked in a whisper.

I reached back for Kydrus and pulled him forward. "Kydrus, I'd like you to meet my new friend, Cassie. Cassie, this is Kydrus," I introduced them.

Kydrus dropped to one knee, his fully charming smile on, lifted her little hand, and kissed her knuckles. "It's nice to meet you, Cassie."

She looked like she was going to explode with joy.

Kydrus stepped aside for Amrynn, then Ryul, then Venali, then Durlan.

When it was Daniel's turn, she tensed.

I squatted down and said, "He's just a big teddy bear. I bet he'd even shift for you."

Her eyes widened.

He knelt and kissed her knuckles. "Hello, Cassie. It's an honor to meet you."

"Daniel, sir, can I see your bear form?" she asked.

"Don't be frightened, okay?" he said.

She nodded.

He stepped behind me and shifted and then peeked his giant furry head around my legs.

Cassie gasped. Then, she reached out a shaky hand, and Daniel licked it, which made her laugh.

I squatted and waved her closer. I pointed to the side of his neck. "This is the softest spot." I buried my face in it and then leaned back.

Without hesitation, she stuck her face in his fur. "It's so soft," she gasped.

I grabbed Myrin and pulled him down. "This is Myrin," I told her.

He smiled. "Hello, Cassie."

She took a step closer to him and tilted her head to the side as she examined him. "Your teeth are sharp like mine."

"Oh?" he asked.

She opened her mouth, showing of her sharp canines.

"Those do look sharp," Myrin said. "And pretty."

Cassie blushed.

He reached out and took her hand, the tension in the air was palpable, then he gently and slowly brought it to his lips to kiss her knuckles. "I hope you'll save me a dance at the ball," he said.

She nodded vigorously and then threw her arms around my neck in a hug and ran back the way she had come. "Mama! I met the queen and her consorts. Can we go to the ball? I want to dance with Myrin."

People had gathered around and when I stood, many introduced themselves.

I needed to give Cassie a gift for breaking the tension.

When we finally left, I felt good about the day. I twirled my flower as we headed to our room, smiling.

"Elara made a friend," Kydrus said.

"Myrin got a date," I said with a chuckle. "I'll have to fight her to dance with him."

Myrin laughed.

"I hope tomorrow won't be as bad," I said and felt my smile slip.

"It'll work out," Durlan assured me.

I scowled at him. "You're only saying that because we're going to Adlin tomorrow."

He smiled. "Maybe."

"Could you stop making me shift on command?" Daniel asked softly. "I feel like entertainment."

I stopped and spun to face him. "I'm sorry. I didn't—"

He covered my mouth with his hand for a second. "I know. You are just showing them I'm not human."

"Did I overstep having Cassie touch you?" I asked, feeling like a total jerk.

"Had it been an adult, yes, but not for that little girl."

Daniel kissed my cheek. "It's okay. I didn't mind today, but don't feel like doing that at each place."

The guilt didn't go away. "Okay. I'm sorry."

He linked our hands and tugged me into our bedroom. "Come on, we've been waiting all day to get you out of that dress."

"It needs to be washed," I said and twirled the skirts which were coated in dust.

"Yet another reason it needs to come off," Myrin said and began unlacing it.

ADLIN AND VLINK WENT EXTREMELY WELL. NO ONE yelled rude things and everyone was excited to meet Myrin and Daniel.

As we prepared to go to Linta, my hands shook. The last time I had been there for more than a couple of hours was the night I had been pushed off the cliff.

Kydrus wrapped his arms around me. "It's okay. I'm going to be at your side the entire time."

"What if they won't accept me?" I asked in a whisper. "What if they—"

"I will handle them," Kydrus assured me, squeezing me tightly.

"Do you think my home...is there?" I asked.

He nodded. "Do you want to see it?"

I nodded.

"After you visit the people, we will go by, okay?" he said.

"Okay," I agreed.

We teleported into the field, just outside of the city.

I lifted my dress with trembling hands as we stepped onto the road.

"Why is she so nervous?" I heard Daniel ask.

"She was an outcast here and the others tended to pick on her," Kydrus said. "They challenged her to fight almost daily."

Not almost...every single day. He just didn't know about all of them.

I took a breath.

That girl wasn't me anymore. I was different now. Stronger. And I had consorts that never left me lonely.

As soon as I walked into Linta, people began whispering and saying my name. Some called out to Kydrus.

Once in the town square, I nailed the invitation to the board Kydrus had installed a few years after I had moved there.

A group stood behind me.

"This is your invitation to a ball I am hosting," I said and turned to face them. "I wanted to personally invite you."

Smiles were not expected and yet that was what I got.

"It's good to see you," Lansia said. She had given me work in her shop occasionally.

"We always knew Kydrus was going to snag you," Tara said from my right.

"Everyone saw how he pined for you, even when you were too afraid," Simon said.

Then, as if a dam broke, they came forward and hugged and congratulated me.

Halfway through, I was crying.

Four women rushed forward and enveloped me in hugs.

When I finally got my emotions under control, I talked with them and told them some of my journey.

They shook hands with all of my consorts, smiling even when meeting Myrin.

"I didn't expect this," I whispered to Kydrus.

He kissed my forehead. "I know, my love. Honestly, I didn't either."

"Aren't they the cutest couple?" Tara gushed.

Heat rushed to my cheeks.

Everyone laughed.

Just before sunset, we walked to my old house. I let my fingers trail along the tree trunks and closed my eyes.

The door was closed, but not locked. When I pushed it open, I found the inside untouched.

The guys looked in, scowling. There wasn't enough room for them all to fit.

"Whenever I lay in this bed," I whispered and ran my fingers along the dusty cover. "I wondered if I would be alone my entire life." I looked up at them and smiled. "I wish I had known how happy I would end up and how loved I would be."

Kydrus pulled me out of the house so they could all touch me. "You'll never be alone again," he whispered.

My chest hurt at his words because that may not be true. If Amara and I separated, she might take them.

How would I explain the disappearance of my consorts to Minloa?

I pulled free. "Don't make promises you can't keep," I whispered. Going back into my house, I looked around to see if there was anything I wanted to take.

There was very little and most items were just necessities for the room.

I walked out and headed to the falls.

Kydrus grabbed my hand and stopped me when I neared the edge. "I'd rather you didn't fall a second time."

"I didn't fall the first time. I was pushed," I said, but stayed where I was. Tilting my head back, I looked up at the stars. "I played with the stars often here."

"That explains why that constellation is different," Kydrus said.

I spun and glared. "I always returned them to their proper places."

He smirked, and I realized he had said that to rile me up on purpose.

"Let's go home," I said.

Would the castle feel like home without them?

I didn't think so.

CHAPTER 23

ELARA

"The last god is the god of animals," I told Amara as I dreamed and looked at her in the mirror as we always did.

Her eyes widened. "Yes. Where has he gone?"

I shrugged. "Your guess is as good as mine, or better actually."

"Maybe he's been absorbed already," she whispered.

"Possible," I said.

"Well, let's assume that's a dead end," she grumbled.

"The ball will be interesting," I mumbled.

She smiled. "It will be good for Minloa."

"And it could be my last celebration with them," I whispered.

"I do not want you left alone," she said.

"They're yours first," I said.

"They love us both."

I nodded.

"With the container, we should be able to defeat him. However, I need you to practice with your own magic, not using mine."

"Okay," I said.

"It will likely take both of us at full power to seal him," she said. "Work on your stamina."

I huffed. "I hate running."

She chuckled. "A necessary evil, I'm afraid."

"Anything else?" I asked.

"That's all for now. Oh, wait. Remember to enjoy this time with the guys. Not just for yourself, but for them. If the worst happens, they'll likely be devastated after the battle and it will take them time to recover. They should have good memories from this time with you to draw on."

I nodded. "Understood."

Our dream ended, and I was thrust into another.

Darkness surrounded me.

"Hello?" I called out.

"You are not Amara," the dark god said.

I froze. "No, I'm not."

"You have a lot of magic. I could be even more powerful if I had you," he said.

"You already know my answer to that."

Heat exploded to my left.

"Your exposure to Amara has made you insolent and put barbs on your tongue. I should cut it out," he snapped.

"Why do you want Amara so badly?" I asked.

"She's mine. She belongs to me. We were supposed to become one, but those other meddling peons made those *boys*."

"Would you let me trade for her place?" I asked.

He was quiet a moment. "You want to trade places with her? Become mine in her place?"

"If you swore to leave her and her consorts alone for eternity, yes," I said.

"That is an offer I must think about," he said.

The dream dissolved, and I woke to seven growling mates.

"What?" I asked.

"You weren't speaking to Amara. We could sense the evil," Myrin said.

I nodded. "Once Amara ended our meeting, he grabbed me."

"What did he say?" Durlan asked.

I stood and stretched. "The usual. I want Amara. Those boys distracted her. Blah. Blah. Blah."

"You mumbled, 'for eternity.' What does that mean?" Daniel asked.

I tensed. I couldn't lie. What could I say? Silence was my only option.

Silence gained me growling.

I opened my wardrobe and debated what to wear and then remembered I had to start running. With a sigh, I changed into my training clothes.

"What are you doing?" Ryul asked.

I put my hair into a ponytail and smiled. "Going for a run. Who wants to join me?"

"Pass," Venali, Durlan, and Amrynn said at the same time.

I snickered. "You old men need your rest?"

"Yes," Venali said.

I skipped to him and kissed his cheek. "Okay. We'll be back soon. Running is not my favorite."

"I'll make breakfast for your return," Durlan said.

"Muffins?" I asked with wide, pleading eyes.

He smirked. "I can make you muffins."

I kissed him. "You're amazing."

"Let's go before it gets hot," Daniel said.

Ryul was still in bed. "I'm going to nap," he told me and waved. "Have fun."

Myrin and Daniel waited at the door.

Kydrus kissed me. "I've got some things to do. Have fun."

I rolled my eyes. "I'm sure this will be loads of fun."

I glanced back at the five staying behind. Why did I get the feeling they were up to something?

"Come on," Myrin said and gently pushed my back.

We used the back door and started a slow jog around the castle.

The three of us were quiet, but I didn't doubt they had a billion things going on in their heads.

Once I was warmed up, I pointed at a tree a ways down the street. "Race?"

Daniel and Myrin both smiled.

"Go," I yelled and ran as fast as I could.

They passed me in a blink, and ran neck and neck towards the tree.

Myrin raised his arms and circled the tree. "Winner," he yelled.

I finally caught up and leaned against the tree. "You guys are stupid fast," I said. I was embarrassed with how heavy my breathing was.

Myrin pinned me between his body and the tree. "I think I should get a prize," he said and kissed my cheek.

"Okay," I said.

"Tell us what you were discussing with him that involves eternity," he said.

I snarled at him and said nothing.

"You were trying to make a deal with him, weren't you?" Daniel asked.

I dropped my head.

"Elara," Myrin growled and his grip on my waist tightened.

"I did not make a deal," I said. That was true. I had offered and he had said he needed time, so a deal hadn't been made yet.

"Don't you dare try to make an offer with him," Daniel growled. "He won't keep his end. He'll just use it against us."

Myrin took my wrists and pulled them up above my head, successfully pinning me.

Daniel lifted my shirt, exposing my breasts.

"What are you two up to?" I asked, wiggling in Myrin's hold, but his vice-like grip gave me no room to move my arms.

Myrin slid his hand down, inside my pants, and slipped his fingers into me. He groaned and growled at the same time. "Always so wet."

Daniel bent and took a nipple into his mouth, sucking on it.

"If someone sees us," I whispered, my breath coming in pants as the pressure in my core built.

Myrin leaned forward, his mouth over mine, and said, "You should be quiet then."

Daniel lavished my breasts with attention while Myrin's fingers brought me to orgasm again and again. Each time I wanted to cry out, Myrin kissed me and swallowed my sounds.

My legs shook, and I wasn't sure I could walk back.

Myrin withdrew his hand and Daniel pulled my shirt down.

I arched a brow. "What about you two?"

"We'll handle that later," Daniel said.

I took a step and teetered.

Myrin picked me up with a chuckle.

"Don't be so smug," I mumbled.

We returned, grabbed clothes, and went to shower.

As soon as the water hit me, Daniel pinned me to the wall, his erection squished between us. "Here, you can scream as loud as you want," he whispered in my ear.

Myrin's gaze burned as he stepped into the water, eyes focused on mine.

I watched the water slide along his muscles. My dark mate.

Daniel lifted me and then slid inside, making me moan as he filled me.

Watching Myrin touch himself while Daniel pumped in and out of me was a huge turn on, and I screamed my orgasm within minutes.

Daniel withdrew and set me on my feet, but kept his arm around my upper body, so my breasts stayed smooshed against his chest.

Myrin gripped my hips and slammed into me from behind, fully burying himself in one move.

As Myrin moved, Daniel reached down and rubbed me.

"What deal were you making with *him*?" he asked.

I growled.

He brought me right to the precipice of orgasm and then stopped. "What deal, Elara?"

Myrin didn't stop and I screamed that orgasm, but I wanted my other one.

"It doesn't matter," I panted. "He's probably not going to take it."

His fingers moved again.

So close.

So close.

They stopped.

"What was the deal?" Daniel asked.

Growling, reached to finish it myself, but Myrin took both of my hands and held them in one of his, behind my back.

Daniel started again, and I felt ready to pop. My head was spinning and my body ached for the release.

Myrin sped up, as did Daniel.

If I didn't answer, they would stop. I had to finish. I was so close.

"What deal?" Myrin asked.

They started to slow, and I yelled, "Me."

Finally, they let me finish and I swore it was the hardest orgasm I had ever had. It was so intense, I just opened my mouth and no sound came out.

Myrin and Daniel grunted and I realized Daniel had been touching himself the whole time.

Slumped against them, I let the aftershocks roll through me.

Neither spoke.

We washed, dressed, and headed to the kitchen in silence.

Coerced or not, I smiled and felt satisfied.

Inside the kitchen, the rest of my consorts whispered to each other while Durlan baked.

I hopped up onto a counter and watched.

"Muffins will be ready in five minutes," Durlan said, looking over and smiling at me.

"What else are you making?" I asked.

He looked at the dough he was kneading. "Bread."

Venali and Myrin whispered together, as did Daniel with Kydrus and Amrynn.

Then, they huddled around Durlan and Ryul.

"What are you all whispering about?" I asked.

Suddenly, Venali, Kydrus, Ryul, and Amrynn left the kitchen.

I looked at the door they exited. "Where are they going?"

"To work off some anger," Durlan growled and pounded on the dough much harder than he had been.

Ah, they must be mad about my offered deal. Myrin and Daniel must have told them.

"How are preparations for the ball going?" I asked.

"Fine," Durlan growled.

"If you want to yell, you can," I said.

He tilted his head back and roared, the sound so loud that it rattled the dishes in the cupboards.

"You can spank me later if you want," I said with a smile.

He glared at me. "Do not joke about this. I can't...I can't even..." He roared again and left the kitchen.

"You two haven't yelled at me yet," I said to Myrin and Daniel. "You didn't even growl when I told you."

"We had already guessed what the offer had been," Daniel said.

"We just wanted you to confirm it," Myrin said.

"So, what's on today's agenda?" I asked.

"You don't have anything today," Myrin said.

I smiled. "Awesome."

The timer dinged, and Daniel pulled out a tin of muffins from the oven.

I snatched one and wrapped it in a cloth so it wouldn't burn me. Then I skipped out of the kitchen and to my war room.

Sitting in my chair, I ate my muffin and looked at the map.

When the time came to fight, I would need all of my people to help. He would likely send too many creatures for my consorts and I to handle alone, plus fighting him.

With the powers of the other gods inside him, it was going to be a tough fight.

Even though we had the jar, we still needed to strategize fighting against him.

I walked to the arena and tried to talk to my consorts, but they ignored me, giving me the silent treatment.

With a sigh I said, "Fine. I need to find where Amara and you seven will live after the fight, anyway. I'll be back for dinner."

All seven turned, but I teleported to Pinolt before they could approach.

CHAPTER 24
AMRYNN

ELARA DISAPPEARED and I felt our bond stretched, not just on this planet, but to another. That made sense, since she couldn't teleport on the planet and only to different ones.

"She teleported to a different planet," I growled.

"What did she say before she left? I couldn't hear," Venali asked.

"She said she needed to find where Amara and the seven of us would live after the fight," Durlan growled. He threw his sword across the arena and it buried to the hilt in the stone wall.

I sat and put my head in my hands. I couldn't lose her.

"We need to figure out a way to make them fully merge," Daniel growled.

"You can't *make* them do anything," Kydrus said, and I could hear the frustration in his tone.

"There might be a way," Myrin whispered and paced along the fence line.

"How?" Ryul asked.

"It could kill us, though," Myrin said.

I watched him and realized he was so deep in thought, he hadn't heard Ryul.

"There could be other negative consequences," he said.

Ryul opened his mouth, and I waved at him to stay quiet.

He narrowed his eyes, but didn't speak.

"If we can get them separated...how, though? How do we convince them to separate?"

I had a feeling I knew where his line of thinking was headed.

"She may not forgive us if we die merging them," I said loudly.

Myrin growled and didn't stop his pacing. "I know."

"How do we keep her from making a deal with him?" Daniel asked.

"We can't," Kydrus said softly.

"I can," Ryul said softly.

We all looked at him, even Myrin stopped pacing to face him.

"How?" I asked.

"If I can control her dreams, he won't be able to invade them," Ryul said.

"You can control dreams?" Myrin asked.

Ryul nodded.

"You'll have to change your sleep schedule," I said. "She'll notice that."

He shrugged. "We should set up rotations in case he attacks anyway."

He wasn't wrong.

"I'll just volunteer for each night and the rest of you can rotate," he said.

"That's not a bad idea," Myrin whispered and resumed pacing.

"Have there been any sightings of Feno?" Kydrus asked.

"Not that I've heard of," Durlan said. "I think it is likely that he is lying low until the ball."

"Where he'll likely strike for maximum effect," I growled.

"There may be others who try to hurt her during the ball," Venali said.

I nodded. "Most likely."

Daniel spun, his nose lifted, and then growled. "We have company."

We grabbed our swords, Durlan having to yank his out of the wall, filed out of the arena, and walked past the courtyard and into the Dead Lands.

"Your nose is incredible," I whispered.

Daniel chuckled.

Twenty fae creatures of varying types and sizes stood together, growling and waiting for us.

Venali smiled. "This will be a much better way to work off my anger. I wish there were more."

Ten more appeared.

Durlan sighed. "Venali, stop talking."

Venali laughed and then ran forward with a mighty battle roar.

Daniel chuckled. "I never thought I'd meet someone who enjoyed fighting and killing as much as shapeshifters."

I patted his shoulder. "Welcome to the family."

He threw his head back and laughed and then shifted to his bear form.

Venali had killed a dozen already and he yelled, "More!"

Twenty more appeared.

For once, I wasn't upset at the enemies. For once, I took the gift before us and worked my frustrations out with killing. My frustration of Elara offering herself to him. My frustration of the humans taking me and then Elara prisoner. My frustration at having failed to protect my mate so many times.

When the year was over, I guaranteed there would be a lot more killing still.

"More," Kydrus yelled.

"More," Myrin yelled.

"More," Daniel roared.

The Dead Lands became a battlefield of our pain and frustration. Bodies, parts, entrails, and blood coated over two square miles before we stopped asking for more and sat together, panting.

Then, three giant creatures unlike anything we had seen before appeared.

We all stood.

"That's more like it," Venali said and as one, we charged the creatures.

CHAPTER 25
ELARA

PINOLT WAS as beautiful as I remembered. Lush green grass, flowers, and wildlife were abundant. It was utterly peaceful. Tranquil.

At least it was, until ten goblins appeared before me.

I sighed. "Really? He brought these beasts here? To my untouched planet?"

Standing, I drew my sword.

"Very well," I whispered. "I've got some anger to burn off anyway."

But I didn't want their blood ruining Pinolt.

I sheathed my sword, stepped forward, and let the goblins latch on to me.

Then, I teleported us to Anderelle, specifically the Dead Lands near Klinsot.

My teleportation skills sucked and I teleported into the sky above the Dead Lands.

Below me, I saw piles of dead bodies and my consorts fighting other creatures.

The goblins were biting and scratching me, fueling my anger.

I whistled and seven heads jerked up.

"A little help with my landing, please," I called down.

Drawing on the sun, I used it to burn the goblins, making them release me.

Free, I continued to fall towards the ground.

Myrin got a running start, and leapt up, snatching me out of the air, and then rolled with me tucked up against his body.

We stopped rolling and I stood, brushing myself off. "Thanks."

"What was that, Elara?" he growled.

I marched towards the goblins, who had survived the fall, somehow. The sun's power still coursed through me. "Teleporting isn't my specialty," I said and raised my hand. The sun's powers left my hand to incinerate the goblins before me.

Sweat dripped down my neck and back.

"I didn't realize the Dead Lands were so hot," I said and pulled my shirt away from my chest.

Myrin scowled. "It's not hot."

My hair stuck to my head, soaked. "It's boiling."

"Ryul," Myrin yelled.

He ran over and scowled at me. "You used the sun, didn't you?"

"I've used it several times before," I growled and fanned my face.

"You have to let the power go," Ryul snapped. "You're going to burn from the inside out."

"I'm trying," I snarled. And I was. It just wouldn't release its hold on me, or my hold on it.

"Would knocking her out help?" Myrin asked.

"No," Ryul said. "Elara, look up at the sky and shoot a flame as high as you can, like you're sending it back to the sun."

I did as he instructed.

Then, I watched as a giant creature was tossed through the flame, burning up instantly.

Two more creatures followed.

Calming down, I focused and closed my connection to the sun.

My body crumpled to the ground once the power left me.

"Elara?" Ryul called.

I lifted my hand. "Alive," I breathed.

The guys sat around me, their breathing heavy, too.

"What were you guys up to? There's like a hundred dead bodies."

"You first," Venali said.

"I went to Pinolt, like I said. While I was there, he sent those filthy goblins after me. I didn't want them tainting my clean world, so I teleported back here with them latched on to me."

"You *let* them bite and scratch you?" Kydrus asked.

I nodded. "It was the easiest way to get them all here. Your turn."

Silence greeted me.

I looked around and all seven had their heads in their hands.

Clearly, they needed a moment to absorb my genius.

One by one, they started laughing until all seven were clutching their stomachs, doubled over.

I waited patiently, closing my eyes to take a quick nap.

When they finally finished, Venali told me about the creatures showing up and how more came each time they asked.

It made me wish I had been here to watch them fighting.

Amrynn rubbed at his chest. "Could you not go to another planet without us next time? It was rather uncomfortable."

I stood without responding and brushed my pants off. "We should head back," I said and headed towards Klinsot, knowing they'd follow.

As I walked, I felt warmth, like a fire, behind me. Once at the road, I turned and saw all the bodies burning with black flames.

Myrin's flames.

The bites and scratches stung and when I resumed walking, I hissed a few times.

"Stop and let Durlan heal you," Daniel said.

I sighed and stopped.

Durlan stood before me, scowling, while he healed me.

"You're scowling," I whispered. "You're going to get wrinkles if you keep doing that."

"I'm surprised I don't have grey hair already," he grumbled. "Done."

I hopped up, kissed his cheek, and resumed walking to the castle.

"What were you doing on that other planet?" Myrin asked.

"I told you. Finding the best spot for a house," I said.

"Planning a vacation home?" Daniel asked.

They had heard me before I left. They knew what I had been doing there. Why were they asking?

"Something like that," I said.

"You should take us there," Ryul said.

I stopped and turned to look at them. "Why?"

"We want to see it," Daniel said.

"Now?" I asked.

"What else are we doing?" Kydrus asked.

Something fishy was going on.

"You seven are up to something," I growled and narrowed my eyes at them.

"Shouldn't we get to see the place we are going to live?" Ryul asked.

My heart clenched, but what would taking them there hurt?

"Fine. Everyone touch me," I said.

They all set a hand on me, and I teleported.

"Whoa," Ryul whispered.

"We were here during one of our jumps back to Anderelle, weren't we?" Amrynn asked.

I nodded.

All of their hands dropped from me.

"It's beautiful," Myrin whispered.

"It is my favorite in our solar system," I said and walked to trace my fingertips along a bright purple flower.

"So, where's our house going to be?" Daniel asked and looked around. "This is a pretty good spot."

Tears filled my eyes, but I avoided looking at them so they wouldn't see. "Yes, this was the spot I had picked for you," I whispered.

"We could put a fighting ring over there," Venali said and pointed to a flat, grassy area.

"A shop there," Durlan said and pointed in the opposite direction.

"Three story house?" Kydrus asked. "We'll need eight rooms and at least five offices."

My jaw clenched as they continued discussing where they would build everything, like they weren't talking about abandoning me.

"Elara?" Myrin called.

His voice sounded far away, faint, muffled.

Hands reached towards me.

"Don't touch me," I said and backed up.

Were they testing me? Were they toying with me? Or did they not care? No, they cared, so what was this?

Tears blinded me, the green grass an ocean of tears.

The pain spread, and I fell to my knees, then Amara took over without letting me stay conscious.

CHAPTER 26

AMARA

MY SEVEN CONSORTS looked at me with varying expressions, but most were pained or sad.

"You are all assholes," I snapped at them.

"You don't—" Ryul started, but I hit him with a blast of power, knocking him to his knees.

"Amara," Myrin whispered.

"She's being ridiculous," Ryul gasped.

"Yes, she's being a tad childish, but she is also preparing for what she believes is going to happen. You want her to be more honest with you and yet when she is, you torture the poor girl. You are not the men I remember. The men I remember wouldn't torment a girl like this, even if she was being ridiculous."

"Help us keep—" Daniel started, but my fury would not be calmed.

I forced them all to their knees. "Do you remember what I told you?" I asked.

"No. Don't," Myrin gasped.

"You all need some time to think. Some time without

Elara or I by your side. Spend some time alone and reflect on what you think is important," I ordered them, and then separated them around the planet. I teleported to a different place, so they couldn't teleport right back to find me, located a nice cave, and sealed Elara and I inside, so they could not use our bond to find us.

I used my powers to place another seal, this one to block the dark god from finding me. Elara needed sleep, the kind safe from *him*. Here, now, she could get that. And I would use the time to strengthen my powers.

CHAPTER 27

KYDRUS

AMARA TELEPORTED US AWAY.

She sent me to a mountain range covered in snow.

Immediately, I teleported back to the spot we had been, but she was gone.

"She sealed Elara and herself somewhere," Durlan said.

I turned and found him sitting in the grass.

"I can't feel them at all," I said and clutched at my chest.

He nodded, his eyes pinched.

This felt worse than when she'd gone to the other solar system.

"Why did we think that was a good idea?" I asked as I sat beside him.

He sighed. "Maybe we *are* just assholes."

"I can agree with that," Venali said and sat.

"How long do you think she is going to leave us here?" Amrynn asked and sat as well.

"No idea," Durlan growled.

"We should try to find Daniel and Myrin," I said. "They could be on the other side of the planet."

"Did we have a collective idiot moment, or what?" Ryul asked as he joined us.

"Yep," we all answered.

"How are we going to find Myrin and Daniel?" Ryul asked.

I said, "I can sense Myrin. Anyone sense Daniel?"

"I do," Venali said. "It is really faint, though."

"How do you guys sense them at all?" Ryul asked with a scowl.

"For someone who is extremely attuned to Elara, you're pretty blind to your brothers," I said.

He shrugged. "Is there a need to be connected? No offense, but Elara and Amara are my only concerns. You guys dying doesn't hurt them, aside from emotionally."

We all sighed.

"You really should have gotten out of that castle more often," Durlan said while shaking his head.

"You're such a socially dense person," Venali said and laughed.

Ryul shrugged, unconcerned.

"Let's split into two groups and leave one person here, in case they show up somehow," Durlan said and stood.

"I'll stay," Ryul said. "Since I can't sense the others anyway."

"Sounds like a plan," I said. "Amrynn, with me."

He stood and brushed himself off. "Yes, sir."

Amyrnn set his hand on my shoulder and I teleported us as close to Myrin as I could. Unfortunately, that put us over a waterfall.

"Shit," I gasped.

Amrynn sighed right before we fell into the water.

Surfacing, I wiped the water from my face and searched for shore.

Amrynn swam in front of me, headed to the left. "This was not how I foresaw today going."

We made it to shore and I took off my shirt to wring it out.

"While the water does look nice, I don't think this is time for a swim," Myrin yelled.

We looked up and found him smiling at us from above the waterfall.

"Never pass up opportunities. We can now say we are the first to ever swim on this planet," I called back, set my hand on Amrynn, and teleported both of us to Myrin.

"Well, I have a feeling we are going to be here awhile," Myrin said.

"Why?" Amrynn asked, pulled his boot off, and dumped water out of it.

"She's sealed herself away and closed our bonds. I believe she is amassing power to prepare for the battle," Myrin said.

"What are we suppose to do on this planet until she comes for us?" Amrynn asked.

Myrin smirked. "Build a house."

We blinked at him.

"I'm sorry, I must have water in my ears. Did you suggest we further piss off our mates?" I asked with an arched brow.

"Trust me, it won't piss them off," Myrin said.

I highly doubted that, but with nothing else to do...

"Okay," I said with a resigned sigh. "But I will totally out you if she gets mad."

He laughed and set his hand on my arm. "Deal."

CHAPTER 28

ELARA

"They're idiots," Amara said as she faced me.

For the first time, we stood facing each other instead of looking in a mirror.

"We agree on that," I said.

"We've been asleep for three days," she told me. "I've been storing magic and now, when he comes, I can separate from you."

"Three days," I gasped.

What were the guys doing?

"I'm going to wake you up now and release our bonds so the guys can find you, okay?"

I nodded.

"Try to ignore them and forget their asshole actions. Your ball is tomorrow and I want you eight to have fun. That's an order."

I wasn't so sure I could do that, but I nodded.

The dream world disappeared and my eyes opened.

Sitting up, I looked around the small cave I had been in. It appeared empty.

The cave entrance was suddenly illuminated, forcing me to cover my eyes.

"Elara," Ryul said and picked me up.

Before I could say anything, he teleported us back to the spot I had last seen the guys.

I rubbed the last of the stars from my eyes and then my jaw dropped.

In what used to be a field, a huge three-story house now stood.

They had built a house while I had been gone.

My other six consorts rushed to us, but I didn't look at any of them.

I just stared at the house they had built.

Tears filled my eyes.

"Elara, do you want to see inside?" Myrin asked.

I held out my arms. "If you want to go back to Anderelle, latch on now."

Once all seven were touching me, I teleported us to Minloa, over Klinsot. As usual, we were in the air, falling towards the ground.

Kydrus teleported us to the courtyard with a chuckle.

I walked away with my eyes focused ahead of me.

They had built a house.

A house for them to live in with Amara.

A house I would never see again.

A house so they could abandon me on Minloa.

I tried to shut my bedroom door, but Myrin blocked it with his foot.

"Elara," he whispered.

"I need to sleep. Tomorrow is the ball," I said, refusing to look at him.

"Weren't you asleep the past three days?" he asked.

Yes, while they had prepared for leaving me.

"You should rest, too," I said. "There are bound to be several attempts on my life tomorrow. It would ruin your plans if I died before the battle with the dark god."

"Are you going to look at me?" he asked.

I shook my head. "No, not today."

Using all my strength and the element of surprise, I shoved him in the chest, out of the doorway, and locked the door closed. Then, I put up a barrier so he couldn't phase through it.

"Elara," he yelled and pounded on the door.

I lay on the bed and fell into a deep sleep.

I TOOK MY BREAKFAST IN MY ROOM AND THEN LET A FEW handmaids help me into my dress and braid my hair.

Once ready, I shoved all of my feelings down into a box and left my room.

Castle staff ran about, making final preparations. I smiled at everyone I passed and went in the side door of the ballroom.

Gasping, I spun in a circle to take in the room. It was decorated in silver and purple and looked absolutely stunning.

Venali walked to me and dropped down to one knee. "Your Majesty." He wore a pair of black breeches and a light tunic.

"You clean up well, Venali," I said.

He stood and smiled down at me. "You look exquisite in that dress."

I stood on tiptoe and whispered in his ear, "Perhaps tonight, you can see how I look out of it as well."

He kissed my cheek. "Sounds like a plan."

I held out my hand, and he set his in it, linking our fingers together. "Escort me to our table?"

He dipped his head. "It would be my honor."

For the first part of the night, we would eat a meal, me and my consorts at the front of the room, and the rest spread out. Then, the tables would be removed and we would dance.

I sat in my throne, which had been moved to sit before the table, and watched the staff making final preparations.

"My queen," Myrin said as he stood on the other side of the table and bowed.

"Hello, handsome. Care to sit with me?"

He smiled. "I would love to." He walked around the table and sat beside me, dropping a kiss on my cheek as he sat. "You look beautiful as always."

"Thank you." I looked at him in a black outfit and asked, "Will you save a dance for me? I know your dance card will be full with your girlfriend showing up."

He chuckled. "I'm sure she will allow me to have at least one dance with you."

Kydrus walked in and scowled at me. "You're not supposed to be in here yet."

I rolled my eyes. "I don't need an introduction."

He sat and Myrin leaned over to whisper to him.

People began trickling in and Venali left to walk around the room. Ryul took his seat after kissing my cheek.

Some attendees noticed us and stood before our table to bow or curtsy and thank me for hosting the party.

A line formed, but I didn't want to rush anyone.

Then, a familiar child's voice yelled, "Elara."

"Make way for her," I said to Ryul.

He hopped over the table and directed the adults to the side so Cassie could run around the table to me.

I stood from my chair and then knelt so I could hug her. "You came," I said with a wide smile.

She nodded with a huge grin. Her hair was braided and she wore a beautiful pink dress. "My parents let me."

Myrin dropped to a knee beside her and bowed his head. "Lady Cassie."

She turned and then executed the most perfect curtsy I had ever seen.

Myrin kissed her knuckles and she started talking to him.

"She worked all night last night on that curtsy," a woman said beside me.

I turned and smiled at a grownup version of the girl. "She's much better than I am. My tutors would have cried at such a perfect demonstration."

She bowed. "Your Majesty, it is an honor to be here."

"Thank you for coming and allowing Cassie to come," I said.

The man beside her bowed. "She's talked about you and your consorts nonstop since your visit."

I chuckled. "We've been looking forward to seeing her again." I pulled out the small box with her present knelt beside Myrin again. "Cassie, I have a gift for you."

Her eyes widened. "A gift?"

I nodded and held it out.

She looked at her parents.

"Go on," her mother urged.

Cassie took the box, untied the ribbon, and pulled out a gem on a necklace. I had put a shooting star inside.

"With it in the gem, the star will continually fly inside, never dying," I said.

She squealed and threw her arms around me. Thank you. Thank you."

"May I put it on?" Myrin asked.

She nodded and turned her back to him.

Gently, Myrin brushed her hair to the side and then tied the necklace on.

Cassie turned and asked, "How does it look?"

"Beautiful," Myrin and I said.

She hugged me again. "Thank you."

"I'll see you once the dances start," Myrin promised her.

She waved and showed her parents the present.

Hundreds more people came and then it was time to eat.

My cheeks were going to hurt from all of the smiling as I watched Seelie and Unseelie eating together.

Yes, things were in motion. Finally.

"Please head to the edges of the room," Durlan said loud enough for everyone to hear.

All of the guests did as he asked, lining the walls of the room.

As soon as it was clear, Kydrus stepped forward, clapped, and everything disappeared.

I spun, mouth agape. "When did you learn to do that?"

He winked and stepped back without answering me.

Several musicians entered and set up, and then began playing music.

Durlan bowed before me and held out his hand. "Will you honor me with a dance, Your Majesty?"

I set my hand in his and nodded.

He led me to the middle of the room, set one hand on my lower back and held my hand with the other. Then, we flowed into a dance.

No one else was dancing, though.

I opened my mouth to say something, and then saw Myrin pick up Cassie and start dancing with her.

"You look gorgeous, Elara," Durlan said.

I smiled. "You look handsome as usual."

A man started to walk onto the floor with a scowl and without a partner, but Venali intercepted him.

"Is that attempt number one?" I asked.

"Seven, actually," Durlan growled.

My eyes widened. Seven attempts on my life tonight.

The song ended and Durlan bowed to me.

Kydrus stepped up and bowed with his hand out.

I let him lead us into the next song.

He leaned closer and whispered, "There is a rumor that we might be able to see you take that dress off tonight."

I laughed. "Is that so? I can't imagine where that rumor came from. Perhaps, it might not be a rumor, though."

"I would very much like to confirm this rumor," he said and then spun me beneath his hand.

"As would I," I said with a wink.

Kydrus laughed, and we didn't stop smiling the rest of the song.

Myrin and Cassie stopped by us when the song ended.

"Are you up for a trade?" I asked Cassie.

She was beaming, her entire body glowed. "Yes," she said.

Myrin passed Cassie to Kydrus and then took my hand and kissed my knuckles.

I stepped close to him. "I'm glad I had something to trade for a dance. Though, you seem to have downgraded."

He smiled, slid his hand up my cheek and around my neck, and then pulled me into a deep kiss. "I love you, Elara."

We began our dance and I rested my head on his chest. Love and pain swelled within me in equal amounts.

"I love you, too, Myrin."

The night turned into a blur of dances with my mates.

Then, women from Linta who I had known while living there asked for dances.

I accepted, and before long, I was dancing with everyone. Smiling like a fool.

As I was spun to dance with a new partner, I had to tilt my head back to look up at him. Our eyes locked and fear and fury filled me.

"Feno," I gasped.

He smiled. In all this time, he had not changed. He looked exactly like I remembered him as a child. "Hello, Elara. You look beautiful. You grew into an exquisite woman."

I didn't want to cause a scene, so I continued dancing with him. "Why are you here?"

He arched a brow. "Did you not invite everyone in Minloa, Seelie and Unseelie?"

"Yes," I said.

When I was a child, I considered him an uncle. He would play with me while my parents were busy and snuck me treats.

"Why?" I asked.

His smile disappeared. "They were hiding the truth about the Unseelie. They and the monarchs before them knew the truth, but kept it hidden and I couldn't let it continue."

No, he had to be lying. My mother was an honest woman and wouldn't have done that.

"Answer me one thing," I said.

The dance ended, but we stayed locked in our dancing position.

"Would you have killed me that night?" I asked.

His eyes locked with mine and I forgot how to breathe. After several tenses moments, he said, "No, that was why I had the tip sent to Ryul and had him take you away. Though, things did not go as planned there."

"Are you here to kill me now?" I asked.

His gaze softened. "Pixie dust, I could never harm you."

Venali's arm shot forward, aimed at Feno's throat.

I pushed Feno back and spun around to face my scarred consort.

"Elara?" he asked, eyes wide.

The entire room had silenced, and my consorts began to converge.

"Stand at guard a moment, please," I said.

Venali straightened and focused his gaze on Feno.

I turned and met Feno's curious eyes. "An enemy unlike any we have seen before is coming. One that has the power to wipe us out."

Several people gasped.

"Will you fight at my side? Defend Minloa from this threat?" I asked Feno.

He dropped to one knee, drew his sword, held it out on

his palms, and bowed his head. "I serve you, Queen Elara. My sword and my life are yours to command."

"Elara," Durlan growled.

I ignored him.

Amara tapped at my mind, so I let her join me, our minds and power combining.

She reached out and touched his sword, which began to glow. "Arise, Feno of Minloa, and become a guardian of Minloa."

The crowd dropped to their knees and bowed.

Feno stood and looked at me with wide eyes.

Amara left again, and I smiled at Feno.

He sheathed his sword.

A dark roiling mass appeared at the edges of my senses.

"Durlan," I snapped.

A woman screamed.

Venali ran out of the room with Myrin on his heels.

"Feno, protect the people," I said and headed after them. "Ryul, stay with him."

"Yes, my queen," Ryul said.

Amrynn and Daniel flanked me as we went out of the castle.

Outside of the castle, just beyond the walls, twenty of the large creatures stood together.

In front of them was an older Seelie man who worked on the kitchen staff. His eyes were pure black.

"Elara," the dark god said from the man's mouth.

I dipped my head. "Bellinor." It was the first time I had said or thought his name, and it stung a bit.

He smiled. "I have come to discuss your offer."

"There is no offer," Myrin growled and his body began to glow.

"You boys are so troublesome," the dark god sighed. "Children, entertain them a bit."

The creatures roared and stepped forward. They were over forty feet tall, had huge claws and fangs, and black matted fur covering their bodies. They had snouts and walked upright.

Venali and Daniel roared back at them.

In a single moment, my consorts and the creatures sprang into action.

The dark god walked calmly through the chaos, his creatures keeping my consorts from attacking him.

He stopped when he stood before me and smiled. "Now, where were we?"

"You came to bargain?" I asked.

I should have been afraid, but somehow, I knew he didn't plan to kill me tonight. Or, at least, not yet.

"Yes," he said and nodded.

The moon was close to full, so it provided us with enough light to see each other.

"I'm listening," I said.

"You willingly come to me, sever your mate bonds with those seven, and live the rest of your Seelie life as my consort," he said.

I arched a brow. "What do I get in exchange?"

"I leave Amara and her consorts alone, letting them live the rest of their lives never being tormented by me again."

"What of Anderelle?" I asked. "Will you stop spreading your darkness here?" I asked.

He scowled. "I allowed the light to reign. It is time for darkness to rule."

I shook my head. "I cannot let you drown my world in darkness."

He narrowed his eyes. "I am allowing the men you love to live out their existences with Amara. I will even agree not to touch Pinolt."

I glanced at the men. They were slaughtering the creatures quickly, and kept glancing at me.

A smile spread as tears filled my eyes a moment. I blinked them away and looked back at the dark god. "I want them to live, yes, but my first priority is to the people of Anderelle. If you cannot agree to cease spreading your darkness, we have no deal."

He glared at me and shook his head. "You are a stupid girl. So very much like Amara."

"It seems we are at an impasse," I said and bowed. "Have a good evening."

The dark god gave me a harsh glare and then his dark presence disappeared and the body of the Seelie man he had been possessing fell.

I caught the man before he hit the ground.

"Your Majesty?" he asked as he opened his eyes, and his body shook.

"It's alright. Just rest a moment," I told him and helped him lie down.

"Elara!" Venali yelled, fear coloring his tone.

I looked up and my eyes widened.

One of the creatures loomed over me, his arm raised, ready to slice me apart with his massive claws.

I had no sword and no time to protect myself.

A dark figure dashed between the creature and I, and blocked the strike with his glowing sword.

"Feno," I gasped.

Feno parried the creature's claws. "Are you hurt?" he asked.

"No," I said and stood. "I just don't have my sword."

The creature attacked and Feno blocked.

Quickly, I picked the Seelie man up and ran to the courtyard. "Go inside when you can," I ordered him. Then, I ran back out.

When I made it to Feno, all of the creatures were dead, including the one he had been fighting.

All six of the guys had blood splattered on them.

"Are you injured?" I asked Feno.

He shook his head.

I looked at the six men stalking forward. "Are any of you injured?"

Myrin grabbed my forearm and pulled me away from Feno and the bodies.

The six surrounded me.

"Don't you hurt him," I snapped.

Myrin's flames flared high on the bodies, and Feno leapt back from the one he had been standing beside.

I growled.

"Feno, return to the ballroom," Durlan said.

Feno nodded.

Before I could speak, someone teleported our group to the bathing chambers.

"What happened?" Durlan asked.

Myrin released me and stripped.

I watched the six of them pull off their clothes, transfixed.

"Elara?" Durlan asked.

I turned, trying really hard to keep my eyes on his face despite the fact that I knew he was naked. "Nothing. Feno told me my parents knew the Unseelie weren't evil, but planned to continue with the rouse. So, he killed them. He said he was the one who tipped Ryul off and that he never would have hurt me."

"What happened between you and the dark god?" Myrin asked.

"You couldn't hear?" I asked.

They all shook their heads.

"He didn't like my terms," I said and shrugged.

"You were negotiating?" Venali asked, walking closer to me.

"Trying," I said, "but he wouldn't budge."

"Let me get this straight. Even after we told you not to... you tried to sell yourself to him?" Myrin asked.

My eyes narrowed. "Did you just refer to me as a whore?"

"What did he offer you?" Durlan asked.

I sighed. "Don't you have blood to wash off?"

"Elara," they all growled.

Ryul walked in. "What did I miss?" he asked.

"Myrin called me a whore," I said.

Myrin groaned and walked into the nearest shower.

"I feel like that is taken out of context," Ryul said.

After everyone was done washing, we teleported to our room.

"Aren't I supposed to say goodbye to my guests?" I asked and hopped onto my bed.

"We explained you helped fight off an enemy and they were understanding," Ryul said.

"So, back to our question," Durlan said, dressed now.

"When I'm old, I think I'll move to the beach," I said.

"Elara!" seven voices shouted.

"He wouldn't agree to keeping his darkness from Anderelle," I said. "So, we couldn't reach a deal. My duty, first and foremost, is to the people of Anderelle."

"You're being really frustrating," Durlan sighed and pinched the bridge of his nose.

"How?" I asked and folded my arms across my chest.

"We want to know the full discussion," Daniel said.

I sighed and fell onto the bed. "He offered to leave Amara and you seven alone, letting you live on Pinolt for the rest of your lives. In exchange, I would sever our mate bonds and be his consort for the rest of my Seelie life. I want you to be safe, but I need Anderelle safe. He said it is darkness's turn to reign."

There was silence, not even breathing audible.

I sat up and all seven stared at me, eerily still.

"Don't ask questions you don't want answers to," I said, stood, and walked out to find a handmaid to help with my dress.

Rosalie, the one I used the most often, popped around the corner, her perfectly curled hair bouncing as she walked. "Need help getting out of the dress?" she asked.

I smiled. "Yes, please."

She followed me back to my room and into the attached restroom.

The guys hadn't moved, still staring at the bed and the spot I had been in.

I closed the door and whispered, "Just ignore them."

She chuckled and began unlacing my dress. "Are you adding that new Unseelie to your harem?"

"Feno? No. Ew." I pretended to gag.

"What? He's very handsome," she said.

"He's basically my uncle," I said and then exhaled in relief when she loosened my dress fully.

"Does that mean he's available?" she asked.

I chuckled. "I don't know, but feel free to find out."

After stepping out of the dress, she brushed out my hair and then gave me a nightgown for bed.

"Anything else?" she asked.

"Nope. Thank you for your help."

She curtsied. "I'll see you in the morning."

When I stepped out into the bedroom, the guys had moved to sitting, but still stared silently at nothing.

"I had fun tonight," I said as I climbed into bed. "It's definitely one of my favorite memories, and I will treasure it for the rest of my life."

None of them responded.

With a sigh, I lay down and went to sleep.

Hopefully, tomorrow would be a good day. First item was to meet with Feno. He and I had a lot to discuss.

CHAPTER 29
MYRIN

WE COULD HAVE LOST her yesterday.

Twice.

If the dark god had lied and said he would leave Anderelle alone, she would have severed our mate bonds to become his consort.

If Feno hadn't been there, she might have been killed by that creature.

My mind was made up, no matter the cost, we would get them to fully merge. I wouldn't lose them.

I wouldn't survive losing them...either of them.

Elara had been the light in the room last night. The sun that people had gravitated towards. She had smiled all night.

She'd said she would cherish last night as a favorite memory, and honestly, so would I.

I had wanted to confront her, to scold her when she woke, but as soon as her eyes opened, she smiled, and I didn't want to do anything to cause that beautiful smile to disappear.

It seemed my six brothers felt the same as we all chatted

with her and mostly watched in enraptured silence while she went through her day with that smile in place.

After lunch, she summoned Feno and took him to her war room to talk. Since she hadn't said we couldn't come, my brothers and I followed and took up seats or standing positions around the room.

She sighed, but then smirked and sat in her chair.

With every confrontation and fight, she grew more confident in herself. Despite being so young and ignorant, she was fast becoming an amazing queen.

Had I not been her consort, I would have tried my hardest to win a place in her bed and then her heart. I would have bowed to her eagerly.

When we had first met, she'd worn mostly fighting attire with high necklines. Now, she wore lower cut shirts, giving us all glorious cleavage views, and dresses. The ones she wore with corsets were definitely my favorite.

"Feno, what do you know about the dark god?" Elara asked.

He sat across from her and treated us like we weren't even there.

Had I been him and receiving the glares Venali and Durlan were giving, I wouldn't have been so relaxed. Then again, he was like an uncle to Elara, so he probably felt safe. He might be safe from being killed by them, but there was still the chance that they'd fight him.

"Very little. I knew there was an increase in fae creatures, and weird creatures, around Minloa, but nothing else. I didn't know you were a vessel for a goddess either."

Elara tilted her head up, looking at the ceiling. "I won't be her vessel much longer."

My heart stilled and for a moment, I forgot how to breathe.

Venali, who had been standing, sat and stared at his fists.

Yes, I could sympathize. We were strong, powerful, and yet we could do nothing about this issue. Brute force couldn't solve this problem.

"Let's get you caught up on all that has happened, so you're and ready for the upcoming battle," Elara continued.

"Could you start with what happened after you woke up?" Feno asked.

She chuckled. "That feels like a lifetime ago. Like someone else's life."

"You are vastly different now," Kydrus said and smiled at her.

She returned his smile and then took a deep breath and began her retelling.

Ryul, Amrynn, and Durlan jumped in to add information she left out or forgot.

I watched Feno, waiting to gauge his reaction.

He didn't seem evil and last night I had seen love in his eyes when he looked at Elara. Still, better safe than sorry.

Feno's eyes grew darker and darker as he listened. Then, the room began to shake. He stood, the shelves rattling and books falling off, and left.

As soon as he left, the room stilled.

"He'll be back," Elara said and relaxed.

I walked to her and knelt on one knee beside her chair. "Do you want anything while you wait?"

She leaned over and kissed my lips, causing a fire that never seemed to die to burn brighter. "Just that," she whispered.

I would slay a thousand creatures to continue receiving those kisses.

I planned to slay a god to continue receiving them.

Feno walked back in, fully composed. He sat across from her again and said, "I have failed you many lifetimes over. There is no way I can repay you. I will stay with you and fight against this dark god."

She smiled. "Your sword will be a great asset for us."

"May I steal Durlan for a bit?" Feno asked.

Elara nodded. "Sure."

Durlan stood, and he and Feno left the room.

"Get him a position here," she said. "He is going to be a key player in our upcoming battle."

Her eyes glazed over a moment and she shook her head.

"Are you alright?" I asked softly.

She cleared her throat and nodded. "I'm fine."

Yet another lie.

"Elara," I growled.

She stood and smiled. "Let's go on a walk. We can scout out the best places to hold our battle."

"The Dead Lands will serve as a great place," Venali said.

"Well, we need to figure out where to set everything up. Come on," she urged. "Walk with me, boys."

We obeyed, but as we exited the room, we all made eye contact and I could see the shared concern there. Elara had a knack for making us worry.

"Fine?" Venali asked as he walked beside me.

I pinched the bridge of my nose. "Yeah."

"If we tickle her, you think she'll tell us?" he asked.

She did hate being tickled.

"Keep an eye on her," I whispered.

He scoffed. "That's all we do."

"And worry," I said.

CHAPTER 30
ELARA

"I WIN," Durlan said and set his final card down.

Everyone, myself included, growled.

That was the sixth game in a row he had won.

"Let's play a different game," I said.

Venali and Ryul nodded their agreement.

Durlan laughed.

I gathered the cards into a single pile for shuffling.

All seven of my mates raised their heads, looking towards the door. Then, Venali, Kydrus, and Daniel dashed out of the room. Amrynn, Myrin, Ryul, and Durlan surrounded me.

Durlan teleported us to my war room. As soon as we arrived, Ryul locked the door and drew his sword.

"Guys?" i asked.

"A large group of powerful people just showed up," Myrin said.

"I don't sense evil," I said with a scowl.

"It is better if we take you somewhere safe until we find out their intentions," Amrynn said.

Someone knocked on the door.

Myrin phased through it and then came back and nodded before pushing open the door for us to see the visitor.

I remembered the first time he had done that and scared me.

Outside stood Tamryn, Warlord of Blythe. He bowed to me. "Your Grace, there are visitors to see you."

I ran my fingers through my hair as I followed to my throne room through the side door. I should have changed clothes or freshened up a bit, but it seemed like they were in a rush so I didn't bother asking. Once seated, I nodded and the front doors opened.

Myrin and Amrynn stood at the foot of the stairs. Durlan stood behind me, ready to give me counsel if needed.

The others spread out around the room.

In through the doors walked ten men in silver fighting leathers with a flower crest on their chests. They had long, silver hair, and pointed ears like me.

They were not Seelie, though. They were long thought extinct.

I stood and skipped down the stairs to meet them on level ground.

The man in front walked with his head held high and a sword with a gemstone with a star in it. Their king.

We stopped a few feet apart. His face stoic. Mine smiling and excited.

The man to his right said, "Introducing, Elryd, King of-"

"The High Elves," I finished.

His stoic expression broke as he smiled. "You know of us?"

I bobbed my head. "I read a lot of old historical texts. We thought you were extinct."

Durlan cleared his throat.

I cringed and forced a stoic courtly face.

"I am Elara, Queen of Minloa, Empress of Anderelle, and vessel of the Goddess of the Universe, Amara."

His eyebrow twitched at my last title, but he made no comment. He bowed, took my hand, and kissed the back of it. "It is an honor to meet you, Queen Elara."

I curtsied. "Likewise, King Elryd." I turned to Kydrus. "Table and chairs, please."

Kydrus snapped his fingers and the pews that had been in the room disappeared. Then, he replaced them with a huge rectangular table with heavy wooden chairs.

I waved at the end chair. "Please, have a seat." I stood next to the head seat and Durlan pulled it out for me.

As he pushed it in, he whispered, "Be wary. We don't know their motives yet."

I sat and smiled at Elryd. A few of his people sat around the table. Amrynn, Durlan, Kydrus, and Myrin sat with me. The rest of my mates took positions around the room in case things went south.

Elryd steepled his fingers. "There has been a rumor that you are fighting against the dark god, B-"

I held out my hand and he stopped. "We don't say his name."

He nodded.

"We have been and are fighting him. I predict a final battle soon."

"How have you been able to fight a god and his creatures?" the elf who had introduced Elryd asked.

"Your name?" I asked.

"Dyffros," he said.

I held out my hand and plucked the star from Elryd's sword and examined it. "Not without pain, but we are holding our own, Dyffros."

All of the elves leapt up.

Elryd smiled. "You're a Celestial Warrior."

I smirked. "I like how that sounds, but I am unsure it fits. I can manipulate the stars and planets, and harness the sun's energy."

He nodded and then snatched the star from me and bounced it in his palm like a ball. "Yes, those are a Celestial Warrior's main abilities."

My mouth dropped open, and I looked at Ryul who had his eyebrows raised in surprise as well.

Elryd scowled. "You've not heard the term before?" He put the star back in the gemstone.

"Most records in regards to those with celestial powers are missing," Ryul said. "And Amara isn't one who cares much for titles."

"You said you are a vessel," Elryd said. "Can you prove it?"

"Why are you here?" Durlan asked.

Dyffros snarled. "Who are you to question a king?"

"He is my mate, consort of Amara, and a demigod," I said. "All of my mates are equal to me and are free to speak."

Dyffros scowled and quieted.

"Your mate and Amara's consort?" Elryd asked.

I huffed. "It's complicated."

He turned to Durlan. "We have come to help fight B-"

All of us yelled, interrupting him.

He sighed.

"Apologies, but we avoid drawing his attention as much as possible," I said.

He nodded. "We've come to help you fight him."

"Why now?" Venali asked from the back of the room.

"We've been watching and waiting," Elryd said. "We had to be sure you weren't going to fall to his charms or lies."

I chuckled mirthlessly. "No need to worry about that."

"Our fighters are excellent and with two Celestial Warriors, defeating him shouldn't be an issue," Elryd said.

"Test," Venali called.

I sighed. "Fine, Venali. Elryd, would you allow your strongest fighter to have a match against mine? So we might gauge your skills?"

He smiled. "Certainly."

I stood and all the men followed suit. "If you'll follow me, we can go to the training arena a—"

"Field," Venali said.

I scowled at him, but relented. "Fine, the field."

Myrin walked at my side, his hands clasped behind his back.

"So?" I asked without looking at him.

"Unsure," he said.

I nodded and we continued on in silence. Once in the open field between the Dead Lands and Klinsot, I stopped and turned to face Venali.

He dropped to one knee before me.

"No killing. No maiming. Test, only. Understood?"

He nodded. "Yes, my queen."

Elryd came to stand beside me. "You seem excited."

I smirked. "The fighting prowess of the High Elves has

been in many fables and texts. I'm excited to see how it compares."

Dyffros stepped into the circle our groups had made and stood before Venali. While Venali was larger overall, I sensed a lot of power from Dyffros.

Venali bowed.

Dyffros bowed back.

"No killing. No maiming. Understood?" I yelled.

Both nodded.

"Begin," I snapped.

Dyffros dashed forward and Venali dodged his punch, spinning around his back, but Dyffros spun as well.

He was definitely fast, possibly as fast as Kydrus.

"Full power," I yelled at Venali.

He growled, backed away from Dyffros, and took a deep breath. When he released it, his body and eyes glowed a moment and then the glow disappeared, but I could feel his power now.

"Interesting," Elryd whispered as he watched.

Venali nodded once and then charged Dyffros.

They started off slow, exchanging blows and blocks, but a few hits later, both exploded into motion.

Each moved so fast, I could hardly keep track.

The sound of flesh hitting flesh made me cringe and worry for them, but I trusted Venali not to take it too far.

Minutes passed and then Venali stood over Dyffros's unconscious body.

The elves didn't even react.

Venali dusted himself off, walked to me, and nodded. "They'll do well in this battle."

Elryd smiled. "You're more than Seelie."

Venali smiled back. "We aren't at full power, but we are able to use some of our demigod abilities."

"I look forward to seeing you on the battlefield," Elryd said.

"Now that that's over, let's get back to business," I said.

"Why are you scowling?" Venali asked as we walked side by side.

"I'm pouting," I admitted. "I couldn't see most of your fight because you were moving so fast."

He hooked his arm around my waist and pulled me close. "I'm sure I could find another elf to knock out and go slower if you'd like."

Why did that actually excite me and sound like a fun idea?

"No," I said and shook my head. "No more knocking out elves."

"Disappointing," Venali said with a sigh. "I was hoping to challenge Elryd."

"No," I said and glared up at him.

He laughed and kissed my cheek. "Fine. Spoil sport."

I shook my head. These males would be the death of me.

CHAPTER 31
AMRYNN

THE HIGH ELVES were long thought dead. Now, they showed up on our doorstep claiming they wanted to help us fight the dark god.

I wasn't sure I could believe them. There was no malice or evil intent coming from them, but it was just so convenient.

"You don't trust them either, do you?" Daniel asked.

I glanced at him as we walked towards our bedroom. "No."

He nodded. "It is good to be wary. I'm really hoping they are here to help, though. We need it."

"He seems rather interested in Elara," I whispered.

Daniel chuckled. "Wouldn't you be? If I was him, I would be trying to find a way into her harem, too."

I sighed. "True, but that doesn't make me feel any better."

He shrugged. "Wasn't trying to make you feel better, just being honest."

"Think she will entertain the thought?" I asked softly.

Daniel stopped and turned to face me. "Why would she?"

"If she thinks we are going to abandon her, she would want someone to keep her company here. The King of the High Elves would be a suitable match for her," I said.

Daniel snarled. "We aren't abandoning her." His eye twitched, and I could sense the hesitancy in his words.

"The possibility is there," I whispered.

"She plans to kill herself, remember? We won't be able to abandon her because she will be dead," he growled and stormed off.

I caught up to him. "We won't let it happen. We will find a way to stop her. Myrin is fairly certain he has found a way to force them to merge."

"I hope he finds something. I don't want to lose her," Daniel whispered and glanced back at Elara who was walking between Myrin and Elryd.

She smiled and laughed at something Elryd said, and I watched several of his men focus on her.

Yes, when she laughed like that it drew you to her like a magnet.

"We can't lock her up just because other men fancy her," Daniel whispered to me.

I growled. "We could."

He chuckled and patted my back. "Glad I'm not the only one who has possessive issues when it comes to her."

I rubbed a hand down my face and turned back around. "They're going to ask to speak to Amara. We should be ready for their attack then."

His eyes widened. "You think they intend to hurt Amara?"

I shrugged. "I have no idea. I just want us to be prepared."

Once back in the throne room, as predicted, Elryd asked to speak to Amara.

Elara closed her eyes and when they opened, Amara looked out. Her body glowed, and I took an involuntary step towards her.

She smiled and Elryd and his elves dropped to one knee before her. "Elryd," she whispered. "You are alive."

He stood and nodded. "I hid a bit too well and lost my way, but I am here now."

"You know him?" I asked Amara.

She turned and smiled at me. "You do not need to worry, Elryd is a friend. He will not hurt me or Elara."

Elryd stood. "If anything, this strengthens my resolve to keep Elara safe. Why haven't you just merged with her?"

"A few reasons," Amara said and cleared her throat while looking away from him.

"Stubbornness," Myrin growled.

"You must be the first consort," Elryd said.

Myrin bowed. "I go by Myrin currently."

"How does Amara know him, but you don't?" I asked Myrin.

"She had gone off several times alone," Myrin said. "She told me about the elves, but since we didn't find them, I assumed they had been killed off as your texts said."

"Elryd and his elves saved me while I was walking the fields of Anderelle," Amara said. "I'd grown weak and he provided nourishment for me and healed me."

"You forgot to eat, didn't you?" Myrin asked.

Her face became stoic. "I don't know what you're talking about."

"She forgot to eat," Elryd confirmed with a smile.

Amara sighed. "Okay, fine. I admit it. I forgot that while on Andrelle I needed to consume the food here to stay nourished."

Myrin pinched the bridge of his nose a moment and then turned and bowed to Elryd. "Thank you for assisting my forgetful goddess."

"Where have you been hiding?" Amara asked.

"Deep underground," Elryd said. "We've been waiting for the right time to return."

"And you believe that's now?" I asked.

He turned to face me. "Your queen has united several continents and races who previously despised each other. She is about to face a battle that will affect the entire galaxy. So, yes, now is the time."

"They trust very few people," Amara whispered.

"Understandable," Elryd said.

"Elryd, Dyffros, and Talron will join you seven for battle strategy discussions," Amara said.

One of the elves in the middle of their group stepped forward. "Me?"

She smiled. "Yes. You are one of the best strategists in the world. You and Durlan should get along well."

He blushed and bowed. "I will do my best."

"I must leave. I cannot merge more with Elara. Protect her, Elryd. She will need your guidance."

Myrin growled, and Amara smacked his arm before she left.

Elara staggered forward a step, but held out her arms before anyone could reach out to her. "I'm fine."

"Did you hear everything?" Myrin asked.

She nodded, drew in a deep breath, and straightened.

"How many are you in your army?" Elara asked Elryd.

"One thousand," he said.

Her eyes widened as did my own. Where were they? They had not come here yet.

"They are waiting for my signal," Elryd said, answering our unspoken question.

"Venali," she called.

He came to her side.

She looked up at him. "Can you assist with accommodations?"

He nodded and immediately left.

Her face paled, and I teleported to her, wrapping my arm around her waist. "Elara?"

Her body was burning hot, and her breath came in short pants.

Myrin met my eyes and bobbed his head once.

I teleported Elara and I to her room.

She went limp in my arms, and her eyes rolled up in the back of her head.

I set her on the bed with a scowl.

She hadn't been having issues merging with Amara lately. So, why now?

Ryul teleported into the room and walked to her. He set his hand on her face and sighed. "She's fine. Just physically exhausted."

"From?" I asked.

"Apparently, secret sessions since none of us have seen her doing anything that would cause this level of exhaustion."

I sighed and sat in the chair beside the bed.

"Or, she's been doing something else," Myrin said as he walked in.

"Like what?" Ryul asked.

"That's what I plan to ask her when she wakes up," Myrin said and snarled.

"How could she sneak out without any of us knowing?" I asked. "With Ryul controlling her dreams?"

We slept in shifts so at least one of us was patrolling the grounds at all times.

"One of the guards said he had seen someone in the woods last night, but they disappeared before he could speak to them. He said it looked like Elara, but he wasn't positive." Myrin sat across from me. "Do you know what I found in the woods?"

"What?" I asked.

"Nothing," he said. "She's hiding something."

I scoffed. "She's always hiding something."

"Like you guys don't," she whispered as she sat up.

"What have you been doing at night in the woods?" Myrin asked.

She scowled. "I haven't been in the woods."

"Why are you so tired then?" I asked.

She shrugged. "Ask Amara. I've been sleeping with you all as far as I know."

Myrin's brows furrowed more. "Wonderful."

CHAPTER 32

ELARA

I FOLLOWED Amrynn to the area that had been provided for the elves between the Dead Lands and Klinsot.

Hundreds of tents were set up and over one thousand elves walked among them. It was a sight I had dreamed of as a child. A wish to see the elven army.

Elryd stepped out of the largest tent and walked to me. "Are you feeling better?"

I smiled. "Amara has been burning the candle at both ends it seems. She likes to keep her consorts on their toes."

"Would you like to take a walk with me?" he requested.

"Sure. Amrynn, can you make sure there is water access?" Before Amrynn could respond to me, I quickly turned and hoped Elryd would follow.

He did. And, he waited until we were out of earshot of his men and Amrynn to speak.

"You seem at odds with them despite saying they are also your mates," he whispered.

I sighed. "It's complicated. We're all trying to come to grips with the possible outcomes after this war."

"Such as?" he asked and plucked a flower from the ground as we walked, twirling it between his fingers.

"Amara sacrificing herself. Me sacrificing myself. Amara and I merging. All of us dying."

He scowled. "Those are heavy outcomes."

I laughed. "Yeah."

"But those are outcomes in any battle. Something else is causing this." His eyes met mine and it was like he could see into my soul.

"Perhaps," I said and turned away, walking again. I headed into the Dead Lands and knelt, letting the sand slip through my fingers.

"If you and Amara separate, they'll have to choose, won't they?" he asked.

Without looking at him I grumbled, "You're rather intuitive."

He chuckled. "When you've been alive for thousands of years and dealt with gods, you pick up on things."

I continued playing with the sand. "I don't want them to have to choose. They were Amara's first. I will die long before her, her being immortal and all."

"Which is why sacrificing yourself sounds ideal." He sat in the sand beside me and drew unfamiliar symbols.

"I wouldn't say ideal."

"If they leave and you survive, will you take new consorts?" He drew a symbol of fire and the sun.

I had seen it somewhere before. Where?

"Potentially, but not for a while afterwards."

"Grieving time," he said and nodded.

He went to wipe the symbol away, but I snagged his wrist, halting him.

"What is that? I've seen it before." I looked up into his eyes, finding his bright with interest.

"It's a Celestial Warrior symbol." He drew another symbol, this one related to the moon.

"My mother had these powers," I whispered. "Perhaps I saw her draw them."

"You seem surprised to see me playing with the star earlier," he said.

I realized I still held his arm, so I released it. "If I let them go, they grow in size."

"Tonight, I will teach you," he said.

I smiled. "Really?"

He nodded. "But, in exchange, I want you to consider marriage to me, should you live and they leave. We could unite our people and my people could come out of hiding."

"Consider it only?" I asked.

He nodded again and smiled wide. "Yes."

Elryd was handsome, powerful, and a Celestial Warrior like me. He was also a king. Marriage to him would be politically brilliant. Could I do it if they left?

I nodded. "Very well."

He stood and dusted off his pants and then held out his hand for me. "We should return."

I let him pull me to my feet and brushed my pants off. "Have you spoken to Durlan yet?"

He shook his head, the silver strands sparkling in the sunlight. "I'll head there now."

Amrynn stood at Elryd's tent, arms folded and a scowl on his face.

Elryd bowed to me and then turned towards the castle.

Once gone, Amrynn stepped forward. "What did he want to talk about?"

I wrapped my arm around his, letting my hand slid along his upper arm and the muscular bicep. He'd bulked up a bit the past year. "He's going to teach me how to use my magic more." I leaned my head against his shoulder as we walked away from the elves.

"He propositioned you, didn't he?" he asked.

"He just asked for me to consider marriage to him, should I survive and you all leave with Amara."

Amrynn stopped and pulled me into a hug. "My love, I will not abandon you. I promised you wouldn't be alone ever again and I meant it."

Tears sprang to my eyes, and I gripped the front of his shirt. "You're hers first, plus, she will outlive me."

"My body and sword are yours. I wouldn't be able to live with myself knowing you were alone here."

"I wouldn't be alone if Elryd married me," I whispered.

Amrynn growled, the rumble vibrated against my face, pressed into his chest. "No. You're mine, Elara. You've been mine since the day I saw you pull a star from the sky." He lifted my chin and kissed me tenderly. "You can't get rid of me so easily. Our souls were destined to bond even without Amara's interference. You are mine and I am yours, end of story."

I rubbed my face against his shirt to wipe off the tears. "I love you, Amrynn."

He kissed the top of my head. "I love you, too. Always will."

CHAPTER 33

DURLAN

ELRYD KNOCKED on my open office door as he stepped inside. "Busy?"

He had his long, silver hair tied back, exposing his pointed ears and sharp features. Something about him screamed predator despite his non-threatening appearance.

"I'm always busy, but I've been expecting you." I waved at the chairs in front of my desk with a smile. "Have a seat."

He moved with a fluid grace that betrayed his age and fighter's training. Although we hadn't seen him fight, I had no doubt that he would hold his own against any of us.

"Elara told me she's considering sacrificing herself. How do you plan to stop her?" he asked.

My eyes widened and I stood dumbfounded for a moment. "She told you that?"

He set his hands in his lap and smirked. "Among other things."

I suppressed a growl. His attitude drew out my possessiveness. Why would she talk so openly with him? A stranger?

"How do you plan to stop her?" he asked again.

I set and met his gaze. "We want them to combine permanently."

"Amara seems against that idea," he said.

I nodded. "Both are."

"What if your plan fails?" he asked.

I let my shoulders sag. "I'm going to be honest with you."

He smiled. "Please."

"We have no idea. We all would sacrifice ourselves to keep Elara safe. Same with Amara. My plan is to keep at least two of us close to them during the battle. Amara hasn't separated from Elara and I'm not sure she can. If she can, that will be when Elara sacrifices herself."

He nodded. "Most likely."

Amrynn charged into the office, his eyes glowing with fury. Before I could stop him, he punched Elryd and tossed him across the room.

I got between them, pushing against Amrynn's chest to stop him from pouncing on Elryd.

Elryd stood and brushed himself off like nothing had happened.

"Amrynn," I snapped. "What are you—"

"Keep away from her," Amrynn growled, snarling to show off his canines. "King or not, I will tear your fucking head off if you mess with her mind anymore. She's mine."

I was totally in the dark about what happened, but grasped the basic situation.

"I'm not messing with her head. She told me of the possibility of you leaving. Only a fool would pass up the chance to ensure a potential courtship with her." Elryd shrugged. "If you were in my place, you would do the same."

"There is no possibility of me leaving," Amrynn snarled. "Elara is mine and I will stay at her side until she breathes her last breath."

Elryd eyed him skeptically. "You'll leave Amara for Elara?"

"Yes," Amrynn said with no hesitation.

My eyes widened. We had all been thinking about it, but Amrynn was the first I'd heard with such a decision.

"Same," Venali said from the doorway.

Elryd shrugged. "Then you have nothing to fear from me. If you don't abandon her, she won't need to consider me. Can we get back to discussing how to keep her alive?"

"Amrynn, leave," I whispered.

He stood snarling at Elryd still.

I looked at Venali for help, but he was glaring at Elryd, too.

Magic help me, how could I get them to leave?

Myrin pushed past Venali and looked around the room. "What's going on?"

"Amrynn and Venali were just leaving," I said and pushed against Amrynn's chest.

He growled, eyes locked on Elryd, but backed up.

Once Amrynn and Venali left, I shut and locked the door. "I'm sorry," I said to Elryd as I returned to my chair behind the desk.

Elryd righted his chair and sat. "No need to apologize. I expected at least one of you to threaten me at some point."

Myrin arched a brow as he sat next to Elryd.

"What happens to you seven if Elara dies?" Elryd asked.

"Our bonds are broken, which will momentarily stun us," I answered.

He tapped his finger on the arm of the chair. "So, we should have at least one of my men with you to protect you if she does sacrifice herself."

Myrin's eyes narrowed. "She won't be sacrificing herself."

Elryd looked at him. "You have a plan to stop her?"

"Merge," Myrin said.

I cocked my head as I looked at him. Something was off with Myrin.

"If that doesn't work?" Elryd asked.

"Will," Myrin said.

"Myrin," I whispered.

He looked at me and the rage in his eyes caught me off guard.

I sighed. "Even you?"

Myrin took a deep breath, closed his eyes as he did, and let it out. When he opened his eyes again, the rage was gone. "Apologies. You're the first true threat we've dealt with in a while."

Elryd smiled. "Thank you."

"Amara has been doing something without even Elara's knowledge. I think she's been separating from Elara, preparing for their plan to seal him."

"Which bodes well for your plan to force them to merge," Elryd said.

Myrin nodded.

"Amara asked me to protect Elara, which leads me to believe she plans to sacrifice herself." Elryd chuckled mirthlessly. "You boys have your work cut out for you. Not only do you have to fight a god and his monsters, you have to keep your mates from killing themselves."

"Sacrificing," I corrected.

He shrugged.

"Shall we move on to discussing the battle itself? I'll fetch the two Amara picked," Elryd said.

I spread the map out on my desk and pulled the wooden triangles we used as troop markers from my top drawer in preparation of our meeting.

Myrin sighed and dropped his head back. "She's making me crazy."

I chuckled. "Understatement of the century."

"Let's hope these elves can help us enough to save them," he whispered.

I nodded. "All we have is hope at this point."

CHAPTER 34

RYUL

THE FURY I sensed led me to the training arena where I found Amrynn and Venali sparring. Both were covered in sweat and snarling, though from the way they interacted it didn't appear the snarls were meant for each other.

I sat atop the fence. "What's up?" I asked loud enough for them to hear me.

They broke apart to turn towards me.

"Trying to quell our murderous desire," Venali said.

I arched a brow. "Towards?"

Amrynn growled. "Elryd."

Well, that was fast. He had not been here a full day yet and they already hated him. What had he done to anger them so much?

"He's trying to take Elara," Venali said.

Those words unleashed a torrent of emotions in me. With a deep breath, I squashed them.

"How?" I asked.

"You're overreacting," Elara said from behind me. She

climbed up to sit beside me. "He only asked for consideration should you all leave."

"I'm not leaving," Venali said.

Pain flashed across her face so fast I almost missed it. She smiled warmly. "Then you have nothing to worry about."

"You don't believe them," I whispered.

"I believe that is how they feel currently. You all also built a house while we were separated."

"That's not—"

Amrynn cut me off. "Amara abandoned us for days. We were bored."

"I promised to be by your side," Venali said as he walked closer.

"That was before you had your memories," she said. She waved her hands. "This doesn't matter. It is all just possibilities of possibilities. Nothing will be decided until after the battle."

"I'm not going to let you sacrifice yourself," Venali said and set his hand on her leg.

She smiled, hopped off the fence, and turned away from us. "You'll try, my loves. You'll try."

We watched her go and the way she spoke, like it was a certain outcome, terrified me.

As a child, whenever she formed a plan, nothing got in her way. She accomplished it even against the greatest of odds. Would this be the same?

Daniel snapped his fingers in front of my face. "Hey."

I blinked and then scowled at all of my brothers now in the arena. When had the others arrived? "What?"

"Time for food," Daniel said.

"Where's Elara?" I asked and jumped down.

"Training," Durlan said.

Amrynn and Venali growled.

Durlan sighed. "Enough, you two."

"Where?" I asked.

Durlan pointed outside.

I walked that direction and felt the others follow.

It took two seconds to find her.

She stood in the black night, holding a star in her hands, a look of pure ecstasy on her face.

It made my heart skip a beat, and my dick twitch in my pants.

Gods, she was perfect.

Elryd clapped and after she returned the star to the sky, she hugged him.

Several growls sounded behind me.

"Easy," I muttered. "As much as we hate this, he is best suited to teach her."

"He could teach her without legs," Venali said.

My lips twitched up into a smile. The big man wasn't wrong.

"Maybe after the battle," I offered.

Elara's body began glowing, and my feet moved before my mind registered why. She was using the sun again.

I couldn't let her burn up. Last time had been scary enough.

As I neared, I realized she was much more in control, so I stopped.

"Think of it as a living thing. A pet. Treat it with respect and it won't burn you," Elryd said.

Elara cupped her hands as though holding a ball between them. A small sun burst into existence between them.

Elryd beamed. "Perfect. Now, throw it as far out into the Dead Lands as you can."

She turned and chucked it.

We all watched, our breaths held.

The light disappeared in the distance.

"What?" Elara asked, disappointment lacing the one word heavily.

Then, a huge explosion from the spot she had thrown it lit up the night. The shock wave knocked us all back. The night was dark again, save for the lights dancing in my vision.

Elryd created a source of light and tossed it up into the sky to show the destruction.

A huge crater at least two hundred feet wide with a smoking center was now in the place she'd thrown the sun ball.

"Well, that's going to hurt to get hit by," Myrin said.

I smirked. "Good thing she's on our side."

"Anyone else incredibly turned on?" Venali asked.

"Yep," all of us responded.

"Let's snag our mate and congratulate her on her new ability," Durlan said.

We snagged her and teleported to our room.

How did she keep getting sexier?

CHAPTER 35
ELARA

I woke sore and happy.

Apparently, the way to turn my mates on was to destroy things. We had missed dinner, and my stomach was displeased to say the least.

Trying to get up proved impossible. Partly because of my sore body and partly because of the arms and legs piled on me.

"Food," I begged.

A few stirred, but none moved.

"Food," I begged louder.

"Yes, my queen," Venali said with a yawn and stood.

I watched his toned ass as he walked to the dresser and grabbed clothes.

One day, I would love to have a naked party, so I could spend all day admiring them.

He winked at me like he had heard my thoughts and then left.

Daniel pulled me into his arms and cocooned his body around mine.

I nestled into him, laying my head on his large bicep. Soon, I would need to leave for training, but we were all trying to take advantage of times like this. We had no idea when he would strike, and I wanted to have as many memories of them as I could.

"I love you," Daniel whispered.

"We love you, too," I whispered back.

He turned me over and stared into my eyes. "I was talking to you, Elara." He brushed my hair behind my ear and kissed the pointed tip of my ear. "When I first realized you weren't truly Amara, I wasn't sure what to make of you. I didn't think I would fall for you, but I fell so hard I'm surprised I remember how to breathe. I can't imagine my life without you in it. Your sarcastic comments, your beautiful face, your gorgeous smile, and that perky little ass. Everything about you is perfect, Elara. I wake up and my first thought is you. Life without you is impossible."

Tears slipped down my cheeks and I took a shuddering breath. Words weren't coming to me, so I kissed and hugged him.

"You're not supposed to make her cry before breakfast," Venali said as he came back in carrying a tray of food.

"It's a good cry," I whispered and wiped my face.

Daniel kissed my cheek and stood, getting dressed.

Myrin and Kydrus rolled over and tried to scoot closer to me to grab me.

I leapt up. "No, I need food."

"Cuddles," Kydrus said, his voice muffled in the pillow.

I jumped over them and pulled on one of their shirts from the day before. Inhaling, I realized it was Myrin's. "Cuddles are amazing, but if I don't eat, I'm going to die. If I die, then you can't have any more cuddles."

"Dramatic much?" Kydrus whispered.

I scowled as I looked at the bed. "Where's Ryul and Amrynn?" They'd been with us when we'd gone to sleep.

"Probably doing a perimeter check," Myrin said and sat up.

I'd started to turn towards Venali and the food, but seeing his bare chest and stomach caused me to pause.

Myrin smirked. "You won't die if you wait just an hour to eat."

I glared at him and turned away. "Evil. Temptress."

"Temptress? I'm not a woman," he said.

I shrugged and sat at the table next to Venali. "There's not a male version of temptress that I could think of." I grabbed a piece of meat and shoved the entire thing in my mouth.

"Chew your food. We can't have cuddles if you choke to death," Daniel said.

Myrin and Kydrus joined us at the table and we ate our breakfast in silence.

Just as I finished, someone knocked on the door.

Venali opened it and stepped back to let the person in. Elryd entered and stared at our food.

"What?" I asked.

"You eat meat?" he asked.

I nodded.

He looked disgusted. "I see. Anyway, it's time for your training. Are you ready?"

"You don't eat meat?" Venali asked.

"No, we don't eat meat," Elryd said. "We don't believe in killing things for food."

"I need to get dressed," I said and stood. "I'll be just a few minutes."

He nodded and stepped out of the room.

Quickly, I changed into my fighting leathers and slid my boots on.

The guys watched me silently.

"I'll see you guys later," I said to them.

They continued watching me, eating and staring.

Weird.

Elryd smiled at me, and we walked side by side down the hallways and out into the training arena.

"Create a sun," he said.

I focused on the sun while holding my hands towards each other, like I held an invisible ball between them. A small sun formed and gradually grew in size until it filled the space I'd made.

"Extinguish it," he ordered.

I scowled. I hadn't tried that before.

"How?" I asked.

"Imagine the power flowing back to the sun."

I did as he said and beamed when it worked.

Venali teleported to me right in the middle of my training with Elryd, grabbed my arm, and teleported me away.

I was preparing to berate him for stealing me for sex again, not that it would be a serious complaint, but froze instead.

Before us stood at least one hundred shapeshifters and humans.

The alpha I had met on Emortalia stepped forward and bowed to me. "Empress."

Venali turned his head to hide his smirk.

"I'm surprised you are here," I admitted.

She straightened. "Daniel sent us directions. I apologize for not being here sooner, but sailing took longer than expected."

"Venali, do we have more tents?" I asked.

He smiled. "I'll have some prepared."

"Thank you for coming," I said loud enough for all of them to hear. "We aren't sure when the battle will commence, so please stay alert."

Amrynn appeared beside me.

"Can you catch the alpha and her leaders up on the plan?" I asked him.

He dipped his head. "Yes, my queen."

"Empress," Venali whispered as he walked by us.

I rubbed my face to hide my smirk.

"Their teleportation is a rather annoying skill," Elryd said as he joined us.

I chuckled.

"Wait until you get teleported to another planet," Amrynn grumbled and then shuddered.

"Shall we return to training?" I asked Elryd.

A strange sound caught my attention.

I turned and Elryd's hand shot out, catching an arrow and stopping it an inch from my face.

My eyes widened.

He turned and threw it back in the direction it had come from.

Venali roared and teleported from behind me to a spot in the Dead Lands over a mile away.

Elryd grabbed my arm and tugged me towards the castle, but I dug my heels in and pulled free of his hold.

"Empress," a shifter yelled, "you should return-"

I walked through them, headed towards Venali who fought my attempted assassin in the distance.

Elryd walked at my side. "This could be a trap."

I nodded and lifted my hand, drawing a bit of the sun to form a shield around me.

He chuckled. "Not what I meant, but your control has definitely improved."

Amrynn teleported to Venali and they fought together against the enemy.

"Try manipulating the gravity," Elryd said.

"It could effect Venali and Amrynn," I countered. They seemed evenly matched with their opponent, otherwise I wouldn't have cared. I didn't want to be the reason they lost.

"I'll protect them," Elryd said.

I nodded, closed my eyes, and extended my senses.

This was the hardest to learn by far. One miscalculation or slip of concentration and I could kill the person. Or, empower them immensely.

The enemy cried out and then the fighting stopped.

I opened my eyes.

The enemy lay on the ground, struggling to rise.

"Perfect," Elryd praised.

We walked to them and I knelt by him...no, her.

She was a Seelie woman with beautiful lilac hair, but a fierce hatred burned in her eyes.

"Why did you try to kill me?" I asked softly.

"You're ruining Minloa," she snapped.

"Who sent you?" I asked.

"Your mom," she spat.

I punched her straight in the teeth. "Don't be rude. Who sent you? Who empowered you?"

"No one. I came on my own," she said. Blood dripped down her lip and onto the sand from her broken teeth and busted lip.

I stood and looked at Venali. "Kill her and burn her body."

He snarled. "With pleasure."

"You're going to kill me?" she asked, eyes wide.

I arched a brow. "You attempted to assassinate your queen. Should I hug you and let you go? You knew the consequences."

Amrynn set his hand on my shoulder, and I set my hand on Elryd's arm.

Releasing my spell let her jump up, but Venali plunged his sword through her chest before she could move more.

"Why was she able to keep up with you?" I asked.

"I don't know," Amrynn growled and teleported us to my war room.

"Her power was different," Elryd said. He sat in one of the chairs and scowled up at the ceiling.

I realized I still had a shield up, so I dismissed it, and sat in my chair.

Myrin walked in, and his brows furrowed when he saw us. "What happened?"

"Someone tried to shoot me in the face with an arrow," I said and yawned.

He pinched the bridge of his nose. "Could you take it a

little more seriously?"

"Elryd caught it," I said and shrugged. "You should talk to Venali and Amrynn because she was really powerful."

He looked at Amrynn who was still snarling.

My right arm throbbed a moment and adrenaline spiked through me.

"Ryul," I gasped and stood.

Ryul teleported into the room in his chair. He groaned and clutched his left shoulder. "They're here."

Amrynn set his hand on Ryul's shoulder and began healing him.

"At the edge of the Dead Lands," Ryul said.

"Let's go." I set a hand on Myrin and Elryd when he came to me.

Ryul and Amrynn joined us, then we teleported to the elf encampment.

"Prepare," Elryd bellowed.

Ryul, Amrynn, and Myrin took turns kissing me before going in separate directions.

Venali teleported to me. "Ready?" he asked.

I nodded and kissed him. "Stay alive, please."

He smiled and kissed my forehead tenderly. "That's my line."

Elryd's army moved from their tents to the Dead Lands, forming ranks.

Elryd drew his sword and together we walked to the front of the elves.

The humans and shapeshifters lined up behind the elves. With them stood several Seelie and Unseelie warriors, men and women.

"They came yesterday saying they wanted to help fight

according to Durlan," Elryd said.

As soon as everyone was in formation, we started the march to meet our enemies.

He wasn't here yet, which I had assumed would be the case.

I drew my sword, and holding the pommel calmed me. Our plan would work. If it didn't, my plan would.

Now was the time. This would decide the fate of not just Minloa or Anderelle, but our galaxy.

Myrin stood about a mile away from the enemy, his hands glowing black.

I had to resist the urge to run to him, keeping my pace with Elryd.

Our army halted a half mile from Myrin.

I continued on, head held high, only stopping when I was beside Myrin.

"Status?" I asked as I looked out over our enemy.

There were thousands of creatures. Most were fae creatures, but many were odd aberrations that oozed bloodlust and evil. Had he created them or twisted some of the fae creatures?

In the middle of their army were dozens of huge redcaps, easily three times the size of the ones we had fought before.

"Three thousand by my calculations, but I could be wrong," Myrin said. "They caught Ryul and Amrynn doing a patrol. Ryul had dropped his guard and got hit in the shoulder. Not serious, but it pissed him off. Amrynn sent him to gather everyone while he took care of his part. Aside from the sneak attack, they've just been standing there, waiting."

"Waiting for him? Or us to attack?" I asked.

He shrugged.

I sheathed my sword, turned to him, and tapped his shoulder.

He extinguished his flames as he faced me.

I stood on tiptoe and kissed him. "I love you."

He rested his forehead against mine. "I love you, too, Elara. Stay by my side, please."

I nodded and faced the enemy again. "Should we wait or attack?"

Durlan, Venali, Amrynn, Daniel, Ryul, and Kydrus teleported to us.

Those I hadn't received kisses from came to me, and then we formed a single line, facing the creatures.

"Wait," Durlan said. "Let's see what they do."

I shifted my feet in the sand, scowling. The guys had trained in the sand, as had I at their insistence, but most of the volunteers likely hadn't. It would impede them.

It would also impede the large enemies, which would help us a lot.

Venali had the most trouble in our group, so the plan was for him to get into the middle of the enemy so they came to him and he could limit his movements. Kydrus was going with him to watch his back, otherwise I wouldn't have been comfortable with that plan.

"Think there are any distance fighters among them?" I asked.

Durlan nodded. "There are a few who can throw fire among them. The goblins have bows and arrows, too."

"I love you all," I whispered. "No matter how this ends, thank you for loving me and giving me the most amazing life."

"We're all going to survive this," Myrin said confidently.

"And we'll love you until the end of time."

"Always," Venali said.

"Forever and ever," Ryul said.

We stood in silence after that. As time past, I grew irritated. "Should I have brought chairs?"

Ryul snickered.

"You're our queen," Durlan said. "If you wish to attack, we will."

"It's been hours," I grumbled.

"I'm ready when you are," Venali said. I looked at him near the end of the line and saw his excited smile.

I looked back at the enemy and projected my voice, "Leave this land peacefully and no harm shall come to you. Continue this invasion and you will be annihilated."

A spriggan stepped forward, it was only child size, but once it was in front of the army, it grew to what looked like around six feet tall. It's mouth opened and it roared at us.

The rest of the enemy army roared as well. Their combined voices were a cacophony of terrifying sounds. Had I never seen or heard them before, I might have been intimidated. It did still make the hairs on the back of my neck stand.

I held my hands a foot apart before me, drew on the sun, and created a ball of sun power. "Ready?" I asked the men I loved more than life itself.

"Yes," they all answered and began glowing.

I threw the ball, directing it to go farther as Elryd had taught me, since my throws were so short, and smiled when it fell into the middle of their army, right next to one of the huge redcaps.

They looked at the glowing orb and then began laughing.

I smirked and snapped my fingers.

CHAPTER 36

DURLAN

ELARA SNAPPED her fingers and the miniature sun exploded. At least one thousand died, and many more were injured. A few ran around, their bodies on fire, screaming.

The enemy charged and our allies charged forward to meet them.

We surrounded Elara, giving her enough room to fight, but being close enough to step in if she needed help.

As much as it went against my alpha instincts, she could fight and I couldn't stop her. I wouldn't stop her.

This was as much her fight as it was ours, and she played a huge role in it.

My goal was to keep the enemy away from her, wait for the bastard god of darkness to show up, and then keep her and Amara alive. What happened after that was uncertain, but I couldn't think about that now.

Daniel and Myrin each grabbed one of Venali's arms and then used all their strength to throw him at the enemy.

Elara's mouth dropped open. "That was not the plan."

Daniel and Myrin threw Kydrus next and then we moved forward, keeping Elara between us.

"We're going to move through the enemy and meet them," I explained as I cut down a goblin.

She didn't respond, her eyes focused on Venali and Kydrus who fought back to back, slicing apart anyone who dared get close enough.

A huge redcap moved towards them, his movement encumbered by the sand.

Her lip lifted in a snarl, she raised her hand, and she shot a bolt of starlight into the redcap's shoulder.

The redcap jerked back and then turned and roared at us.

"Well, you pissed him off good," Daniel said.

Elara sighed. "Great."

I chuckled.

She shoved her blade into the belly of a spriggan who'd increased his size, and twisted.

Damn, she was so hot.

"Durlan," Myrin growled.

"Don't act like you weren't thinking the same," I said.

Myrin cut down several creatures and then set a group in the distance on fire with his black fire. "I didn't say that."

I chuckled.

"What are you talking about?" Elara asked, dodging the arrow of a goblin.

"They're aiming at her," I snapped and moved closer to her.

"I see that," Myrin growled. "I don't see them, though."

The redcap Elara had pissed off finally made it to us, knocking his own friendlies out of the way to reach us.

Elara smiled. "How's the shoulder, big guy?"

I groaned. "Don't taunt the enemy."

The redcap roared at her and my little, crazy mate roared right back at him.

"I never thought I'd say I got a hard on during a battle, but here we are," Daniel said.

I let out a bark of laughter as I sliced into several trolls. How were they out during the day time? The sunlight should have turned them to stone.

Myrin and Daniel fought the redcap alongside Elara. She darted around the giant creature, cutting into his tendons and keeping out of his range.

The familiar whizzing sound approached.

"Arrows!" I bellowed.

Ryul raised his hands and a translucent shield appeared over our allies and us.

"When did you learn that?" Elara asked as she dodged the redcap's attempt to backhand her.

He winked at her, dropped the shield once the arrows stopped, and returned to fighting enemies in front of us.

The redcap raised its left hand and then swung its right hand, catching Elara in the chest.

She flew backwards, but Elryd was there, and he caught her and steadied her.

Red filled my vision, and I roared at the redcap. Leaping up as high as I could, I stabbed my sword into its chest and then used it to propel myself upwards. Jerking my sword free as I flew up, I jammed it into the redcap's neck and roared right in his face.

It fell to his knees, blood bubbling out of his neck.

The red haze cleared, and I pulled my sword free. Several of the nearby enemies had stopped to stare, wide-eyed.

I stood atop the dead redcap's body and roared as loudly as I could.

A dozen or so turned and fled in the opposite direction.

"Think we could sneak off for ten minutes?" Elara whispered in my ear.

I growled at her. "You're awful."

She rolled her eyes at me and hopped down from the redcap.

With the fleeing enemies, we had a bit of space and breathing room. Elara wiped off her sword and looked around.

"No sign of him yet," she whispered.

We nodded and marched forward, regrouping and getting back into the fight.

"Show off," Kydrus called to me as we finally made it to him and Venali.

Venali was smiling as he killed. I hadn't seen him in a large battle like this in a very long time, and had forgotten how terrifying the brute was.

"Join the fun," Venali called to us.

"Your mates are strange," Elryd said.

"You don't know the half of it," Elara whispered back.

CHAPTER 37

RYUL

I'D NEVER BEEN in a battle like this before. I understood more about my brothers and their knowledge and skills.

Had I not been beside them, witnessing how calm they remained as they slaughtered hundreds of creatures, I might have freaked out a bit.

The most surprising was Elara, though. She got right into the thick of the battle and didn't back down.

Watching her roar at the redcap had been terrifying, and yet pride had swelled within me.

She had grown so much. As much as I wanted to take credit, it was all my brothers' doing. And Amara. Amara definitely had a huge impact on Elara. Partly due to their merging, but also her guidance.

A goblin charged me, sword raised.

I parried the strike and then punched him in the chest. He stumbled back, giving me the opening I needed to cut his head off.

Kydrus pushed my head down and stabbed a goblin

behind me. "Saved your head," he said with a wide smile. "Don't leave your back open. This isn't a one on one fight."

"Thanks," I said, turning to fight a spriggan. The bastard kept changing size, which made it hard to hit him.

I growled my frustration, and he laughed at me.

Venali killed a redcap beside me, practically glowing with joy. "Overhead strikes," he said and brought his blade down, cutting the spriggan in half with one swing. "Doesn't matter if he changes size mid-swing, he'll still get chopped in half."

A goblin leapt at his back.

I opened my mouth, but Venali stabbed his sword backwards, making the goblin impale itself.

Venali jerked his blade free. "It's such a glorious day!"

I was so glad he was on our side.

Two redcaps marched forward, their feet sinking in the sand with every move.

Venali started to move towards them, but Myrin coated them in his black flames.

"Myrin!" Venali snapped.

Myrin rolled his eyes. "There are plenty more creatures for you to fight."

"Leave the big ones to me," Venali growled. He stabbed a weird tree nymph/goblin cross so hard in the chest that its upper body exploded.

My eyes widened.

"Fine," Myrin agreed.

Venali bobbed his head and killed a trio of spriggans racing for Elara.

The enemies' numbers were quickly decreasing while ours was diminishing at less than a quarter of the rate.

Elryd and his elves moved well even in the sand and were well-trained to work in pairs and quads.

Elryd used his celestial powers off and on, but it seemed to me that he was saving his magic.

With *him* not here yet, that made sense.

CHAPTER 38
VENALI

THERE WERE so many creatures to kill and yet not enough. My sword was coated in blood and gore. I tried to flick it off, but then it just got dirty again when I stabbed another creature.

The abominations he had created were disgusting and incredibly fun to kill. The tree nymph/goblin mixes screamed really nicely when I stabbed them.

A giant beast pushed his way through the enemies. He was covered in shaggy black fur, extremely muscular, and had at least six-inch-long claws from his fingertips and toes. He also had thick pointed teeth.

A goblin got in his way and he kicked it over our heads.

I took a breath and my muscles doubled in size, a handy power I'd discovered that helped boost my strength for a short duration of time.

"Mine!" I bellowed and ran towards it. "Mine. Mine. Mine."

"We heard you," Myrin said.

Energy coursed through me, aiding in my speed to reach

him. The damn sand had always been a hindrance for me, due to my weight, but I didn't falter even as it shifted beneath my boots with each step.

The shaggy beast looked at me and snarled.

"Let's play," I said with a smile and spun my sword as I finally made it to him.

He swung a clawed hand with a roar.

I ducked, raised my sword, and let his own momentum slice his arm open on my blade. I used a bit of my special demigod magic to make the cut hurt even more than it should have.

He bellowed in pain and kicked at me.

Leaping up and over his leg and arm, I cut across his chest, landed, and rolled away before he could hit me.

Laughter bubbled out of me as I danced with the beast.

CHAPTER 39

MYRIN

MY BROTHERS WERE INSANE. I knew that, but watching Venali laugh while he cut apart a huge beast was eerie, even for the big guy.

Kydrus, Durlan, and Amrynn weren't much better. They might not have been laughing, but they kept smiling while they killed creature after creature.

Daniel and Ryul were quiet as they fought. Both focused and brutal in their efficiencies.

Even Elara was enjoying it.

I had wanted to scold her for roaring at the redcap and standing on the other one's body with Amrynn, but realized there was no point.

With the exception of Venali, we kept our formation tight enough that any one of us could race to Elara's aid if she needed us.

The feisty queen hardly needed our help, though, it turned out. Bodies piled up around her, blood splattered her face and clothes, and she fought on with a snarl curling one of her beautiful lips.

"You should rest," I called to her. "Save your energy for the main fight."

She growled at me in response.

I sighed and stabbed the troll in front of me.

"She'll calm down in a little bit," Kydrus said with a wide smile, hacking off the troll's head.

A tall, thin creature with brown mottled skin, sunken black eyes, and red tipped claws walked towards me calmly. It's gaze was locked on mine and all of the other enemies moved out of its way. As it neared, the evil it emanated was so intense, even I cringed. "You must die," it said in a guttural voice.

"What are you?" I asked.

It smiled, revealing long, serrated teeth. "A creation with a sole design and purpose of killing you."

Bowing, I said, "How kind of him to admit I'm such a worthy adversary."

"Just another stubborn weed to be pulled," it said with a graceful shrug of its shoulders. Reaching back, it drew two curved swords. "It is time for you to die."

With a flick of my hand, I covered it in my black flames. I didn't have time to waste on this thing.

Unfortunately, the screaming that usually followed that move did not happen.

Instead, the creature smiled and the flames disappeared.

"Well, that's new," Amrynn muttered behind me.

I narrowed my eyes.

Immunity to my flames should not have been possible.

The creature dashed forward with incredible speed, reaching me in no time.

I ducked the first blade and blocked the second with my sword.

We danced, exchanging blows and parrying each other in equal measures. I lost count of the number of strikes once I reached one hundred.

After a strike that vibrated up my arms, we leapt apart.

"I can see why he views you as a threat," the creature said and wiped blood off its cheek. "It's time to get serious."

It leapt forward again, but Elara stepped between us, pressed her hand to the creature's chest, and it exploded in a burst of sunlight.

"Elara," I growled.

She looked back at me, her eyes glowing orbs, and said, "He is here."

A cloud of black smoke swirled down from the sky to the ground in front of us, and he stepped out.

I pulled Elara back so she stood beside me.

He glared at Elara. "You destroyed my creature."

She smiled, her eyes back to normal. "I've destroyed a lot of your creatures."

"Give yourself to me, and I will spare your men," he said.

Elara raised her chin. "Submit to me or perish."

Darkness gathered around him, and he yelled, "I am darkness. I am—"

Elara gathered sunlight around her and yelled, "I am light. You do not frighten me!"

Hot damn, she was sexy.

"You will bow to me," he growled.

"We bow to no one," Elara said, her voice a combination of hers and Amara's.

Ah, my goddess had joined the fight.

He drew up and magic built around him.

Amara took over, her magic built in an instant, and she hit the dark god in the center of his chest with a blast of light.

He staggered, his eyes widening, but sent a blast of fire at her.

I threw up a wall of black fire that absorbed his.

He growled and snapped his fingers.

Dozens of creatures that appeared to be made of darkness popped into existence between him and us.

"Group!" I bellowed.

My brothers finished killing what was in front of them and tightened our circle around Amara.

Elryd dashed into our circle, standing at Amara's side. He weaved his hands around his body in a strange motion. Then, tiny orbs of light popped up around him. He aimed each at a dark creature and it burned holes through their bodies, crippling some and killing a few.

Venali stood beside Kydrus. "Ready?"

Kydrus offered an evil grin. "Yes."

What did those two have planned?

Kydrus clapped his hands and a pile of spears appeared at his feet.

Ryul, Daniel, and Venali each picked one up and then threw them at the dark god.

He dodged a few, knocked one away, and one cut his cheek as it sailed by his face.

I joined them, grabbing spears and chucking them as fast as we could.

Amara laughed and threw bolts of light shaped like spears at him, too.

CHAPTER 40
AMARA

THE SPEARS WOULDN'T KILL him, but that wasn't the point. The point was to make him deplete his magic and stamina to make it easier to seal him.

My consorts hadn't told me this part of the plan, but I totally approved.

Elryd adapted to our tactics easily, and I even saw the king smile.

The dark god roared his rage and flung his magic in a wall.

I threw up a barrier as did Ryul.

The magic shattered Ryul's barrier and almost broke mine.

If we didn't act soon, we would run out of steam and magic ourselves.

"Ready?" I asked Elara.

"Yes."

CHAPTER 41
ELARA

AMARA REACHED INTO A SPACIAL POCKET, and pulled out the jar. Then, she gave me control.

I held the jar and took slow, deep breaths. This would work. It had to.

I took another deep breath and cringed as Amara separated from me.

The pain was intense, making me drop to one knee to catch my breath.

Amara helped me stand and smiled at me. She was gorgeous and despite seeing her in my dreams, seeing her in real life was incredibly different.

"Begin," I said with a nod.

She returned my nod, and we faced the dark god.

His eyes focused on the jar, and he clapped his hands, brining more creatures to fight.

How many did he freaking have?

Amara and I held out our hands, created a rope of light, and secured it around him.

She tapped the jar, activating its magic, and a vacuum began to suck him towards it.

He struggled, digging his heels in, and fighting our constraints. "You are not strong enough. You're weak just like the other gods I absorbed. You cannot seal me," he yelled, but I could see the doubt in his eyes.

Amara and I pulled with all our might. Inch by inch, he drew closer.

The guys fought the creatures, keeping Amara and I free and safe to do this.

Amara's teeth ground together, sweat beaded on her forehead, and her light flickered a bit.

She wasn't as strong in her own body. If she faltered, he would get free.

I looked at the fight around us.

Our allies, my people, and my mates fought against the darkness, but there seemed to be no end to them.

My mates had deep gashes on each of them from the new wave of enemies that pressed down upon them.

Being unable to move about restricted their fighting abilities, and caused them to get hurt.

If this didn't end soon, our side would lose. Minloa would fall to the darkness, and then it would spread across Anderelle and the rest of the galaxy.

No, I couldn't let that happen.

I had to save them. I couldn't let my mates die. I wouldn't survive that.

I had to activate my plan. I had to save my galaxy.

Myrin met my eyes from where he fought creatures and I smiled at him. "I love you."

CHAPTER 42

MYRIN

AMARA AND ELARA HAD SEPARATED, which caused us a dilemma. Who did we protect?

Ryul, Kydrus, and Amrynn moved closer to Elara, protecting her back from the creatures. Daniel and I were closest to Amara, so we protected her.

Venali stood in the middle, smiling and killing.

"Now!" Amara shouted.

Amara and Elara raised their hands and the dark god cried out as a wind swirled around him and dragged him towards the container.

"No," he yelled and clawed at the dirt and any nearby creature, trying to stop his progression.

Amara grunted, her forehead beaded with sweat, and her face red from exertion.

They weren't going to make it.

Elara's eyebrows pinched, her jaw set with determination. She looked around at everyone fighting, at Elryd and his elves fighting, and at Amara, and then her eyebrows and jaw relaxed. She met my eyes, smiled, and said, "I love you."

"No," I screamed. I cut down the creatures before me, but I was too slow.

Elara grabbed the dark god, wrapped her body around his, and they both disappeared into the jar.

"No," I roared and fell to my knees. She was gone. She'd sealed herself into the jar with him, to save Amara, and to save us.

"No," Venali, Ryul, and Kydrus roared.

All seven of us knelt on the ground, our tears uncontrollable as our mate vanished, our bond severed, and our hearts froze.

Elryd and his elves surrounded us, protecting us against the enemies while we were weak.

Amara looked at me, her own cheeks soaked with tears. "I didn't know her plan. She hid it. I'm sorry. I'm so sorry."

There was no way to set Elara free without setting the dark god free, too. Could he hurt her in the container? Would he hurt her?

"Please," Amrynn begged. "There has to be something you can do." He looked up at Amara, clutching his chest.

"Please," Venali begged.

"No, this can't be," Daniel whispered. "She can't be gone."

Amara looked at each of us, the sorrow and pain evident as we all clutched at our now cold chests.

She knelt beside me and kissed me softly. "I love you, Myrin. She cannot be left in there. I can save her, but—"

"You will die," I guessed.

She nodded and sniffled. "I cannot bear to see my mates so distraught. I will bring her back. Will you help me?"

"We don't want to lose you either," I snapped. "Why must we lose one of you?"

"That is that only way," she whispered.

I hugged her tightly. "I don't want to spend another lifetime without you. I love you, Amara. Don't do this. There must be a way for you both to live."

"We cannot merge now. If we both live, the god will be freed and you seven will die," she whispered. "Neither Elara or I want that."

"Don't leave me again," I begged, a fresh wave of tears slipping down my face.

"A bit of me will always remain with Elara. Cherish her and help her. She deserves happiness."

"Amara, no," Daniel begged.

She turned and kissed him. "She will need you to be at your strongest. Our separation will greatly weaken her," Amara whispered.

"Don't," Kydrus choked. "She wouldn't want this. She sacrificed herself for a reason."

"Be strong, my loves," Amara said. She backed up, glowed brightly, and then disappeared.

"Plan M," I snapped and saw the others nod once.

We looked around unsure what had happened to Amara, and then time rewound itself. We watched Elara and the dark god come out, the creatures still held at bay despite the seven of us being at Elara's feet now.

I would not let them do this.

As soon as time began to move again, I stood and yelled, "Together."

The moment Elara made her decision, her eyes meeting

mine, the seven of us grasped hands with each other and our two mates, chaining Elara and Amara together.

Their magic channeled through us, using us as a bridge, and with a burst of light and surge of power, the two women became one.

CHAPTER 43
ELARA / AMARA

ALL SEVEN OF my consorts fell to the ground, their magic drained to fully merge us.

The dark god bellowed and a bolt of dark energy slammed into Daniel's chest.

With a sweep of my hand, we finished sealing the dark god, and sent his container to a distant star where no life existed.

"You fools," I snapped as I dropped to the ground beside Daniel. "What have you done?" Daniel hadn't moved since the dark god hit him. He looked peaceful and even had a small smile on his face. Tears streamed down mine.

"Saved you," Myrin gasped. "Elara sacrificed herself. Amara reversed time to trade places."

"We couldn't lose either of you," Ryul said, tears on his face.

"Daniel?" I whispered and rested my hand on his cheek.

Our link was dark. Our connection severed.

"No!" I set my hands on his chest. He wasn't breathing

and his body was growing cold. "Daniel," I cried and pressed my hands to each side of his face. Tears streamed down my cheeks as I looked at my shapeshifter mate.

CHAPTER 44

MYRIN

DANIEL WAS the least powerful of us all. He had very little magic in comparison to the rest of us. I should have thought about that before we used our powers to merge them.

He was dead. His life snuffed out to save Elara and Amara.

She pressed her hands to his chest and a bright white glow surrounded him as she tried to use her magic on him.

It wouldn't work. She couldn't bring him back to life like she had Durlan because she couldn't give up years of her life now that they were merged.

"Me," Feno said and knelt beside Daniel's body. "Take part of my life."

She shook her head, tears dripping from her jaw. "I can't—"

Feno took her face in his hands and said, "Take as many years as you need. I have been on this planet long enough and I will not sit by while you are mourning if I can change it. I took your parents from you. I will not sit idly by and let your mate be taken from you either."

She stared at him for several moments before placing one hand on Feno's chest and one hand on Daniel's chest. Her eyes glowed bright white and then a white smoke passed from Feno into Daniel.

Daniel's eyes snapped open and he gasped in a breath.

Feno fell to the side, his eyes closed. I watched his chest to be sure he breathed before looking back at Daniel.

He looked at me and asked, "What did I miss?"

I chuckled. "I'll tell you everything later. We still have a battle to fight."

CHAPTER 45

ELARA / ΛMARA

I LET OUT A LONG SIGH, kissed Daniel, and then stood. I looked out over the Seelie and Unseelie still fighting the dark god's creatures despite him being gone.

It was time for this to end. It was time for us to enter a reign of peace.

"Enough," I snapped loud enough for everyone on the battlefield to hear.

Every being froze.

"This battle is over. He has been defeated. Unless you wish to be exterminated, leave now. As Goddess of the Universe, I command you."

Immediately, all of the dark creatures fled, hightailing it before they were obliterated.

The Seelie and Unseelie cheered and some hugged each other. Some even hugged the elves who were stiff, but did not rebuke the affection.

Feno stood with help from Elryd, both smiling.

"What shall we call you now?" Myrin asked and knelt before me.

Smiling, I said, "I've decided to keep the name Elara, due to her sacrifice. And, as promised to us, the goddess powers will be accessible though not always present, and we will live out the next hundred years as Elara. After Elara's one hundred year rule, we will return to the stars."

"And us?" Amrynn asked, standing and moving closer to me.

I smiled. "You go where I go. You seven are stuck with me for eternity."

Taking a breath, I released my goddess powers and stood before my mates once again as Elara, though we were fully merged now, so I was still us, but a bit more myself.

Wobbling slightly, I stepped closer to my mates.

All seven leapt to their feet and reached out to steady me.

Smiling wide, I asked, "Who wants a bath? We're all covered in blood and muck."

Daniel picked me up and kissed me deeply, his tongue dancing with mine. He pulled away, leaving my heart fluttering. "We'll do whatever you wish, my goddess."

A huge thundering overhead drew everyone's attention.

The fading sunlight reflected off the side of a large flying ship. At the helm stood Barry, a smug smile on his face as he flew down towards us.

Most of those gathered stared warily at the ship, unsure what it was or what to think of it.

"Shall we destroy him before he lands?" Myrin asked.

I smiled. "No, let's see what he does. Ryul, a shield, please?" I rested my hand on his shoulder to give him a bit of extra magic, since he'd used up so much of his during the battle.

Ryul lifted his hands and a translucent shield spread out to cover all of our people.

"Surrender the woman to me and I will leave the rest of you unharmed," Barry called through a loud speaker.

"Pass," I said and smiled warmly up at him.

Barry scowled and said something I couldn't hear to the human beside him. Four cannons on the bottom of the ship swiveled around until they were pointed at us and then shot over a dozen metal projectiles at us.

They exploded when they hit Ryul's shield, but did no damage to us.

I waved at Barry with a wide smile.

His scowl turned into a glare and he barked orders at his crew.

More shots hit Ryul's shield.

"May I?" Amrynn asked.

I knew he wanted revenge on Barry far more than I. So, I nodded and kissed his cheek. "Be safe," I whispered.

He smiled and kissed my cheek back. "Yes, my goddess."

He squatted down and then leapt up into the air.

He was nowhere near the ship, so I wasn't sure what he planned to do.

Venali was thrown into the air by Kydrus and Durlan, and then Venali grabbed Amrynn and threw Amrynn with a mighty bellow.

Amrynn tucked his arms against his body and flew right at the main deck's viewing window where Barry stood.

Barry looked at Amrynn with an arched brow, the confusion obvious.

Amrynn drew his sword and with two quick swings, shattered the glass.

The crew inside screamed and Barry ducked down, covering his head to protect himself from the glass falling around him

I thought he would torment Barry. Or grab him and say something. Draw out Barry's death a little bit.

Amrynn did none of that. He swung his sword once more and decapitated Barry.

"Well, he is definitely dead," Ryul whispered.

Amrynn stabbed his sword into Barry's chest, tilted his head back, and roared.

"Toss me," I ordered Myrin.

He grumbled, but threw me up to the ship.

I used a bit of my power to make my landing smooth and stood before the humans who cowered around the control panels. "I am the goddess of this universe. This is my consort. We had a score to settle with this man." I indicated Barry's dead body. "You are free to return to Zenlop. Or, if you wish to continue this fight, we can slaughter you here and now."

"We will return to Zenlop," a willowy man in the back said.

I nodded. "Good choice."

CHAPTER 46

ELARA

I THREW a feast for the entirety of Anderelle, inviting everyone from Minloa, Emortalia, and Eltare to celebrate our victory.

Using my magic, I reshaped the Dead Lands and returned it to a rich and thriving grassland as it once had been. I offered the lands to Elryd and the shapeshifters, giving them a place to live on Minloa, should they wish it. The shapeshifters opted to return to Emortalia, while Elryd and his elves accepted my offer and moved into the Dead Lands, now renamed Amlantia.

For a full day, I danced with my seven mates, ate, drank, and played with my people.

Watching shapeshifters, humans, elves, Seelie, and Unseelie laugh and dance together brought tears of joy to my eyes.

I had done it. I had united everyone. Well, minus Zenlop, but they were an issue for another decade. No, my mates had done it. While I had sacrificed myself initially, their love was the reason Amara rewound time to rescue me.

Daniel shifted into his bear form and became a play structure for a group of toddlers.

I covered my mouth with my hand to keep from laughing.

"You look happy," Venali said as he came to stand beside me.

I jumped up to kiss the scars below his eye. "I am."

He pulled me against his side, squeezing me. "Good."

"Any suggestions on who my heir should be?" I asked, looking out over the crowd.

He turned me so we were facing each other, a smirk making his eyes bright. "I thought we could try making one."

My eyes widened. "Making one?"

He nodded. "The world would benefit by having your blood heir here, when we return to the stars."

"We've been talking," Kydrus said behind me. "And we all think you'd make a great mother."

I stepped back from Venali and folded my arms across my chest. "More consort meetings behind my back?"

He smiled. "Maybe."

Arms wrapped around me from behind. I inhaled.

Myrin.

"If you don't get pregnant, we thought you'd at least enjoy our attempts," Myrin whispered and pressed his lower body against mine to make it clear what he meant.

"I suppose I could be persuaded to try," I said breathlessly.

"There's no time like the present," Daniel said and tossed me over his shoulder.

I laughed. I hadn't even heard him approach.

He carried me into the castle, my other mates following behind, and all I could do was smile.

These seven were perfect and while life wasn't always perfect, I would enjoy every moment with them.

I wasn't just a former slave. I wasn't just a queen.

I was Elara, Goddess of the Universe, mate to seven glorious demigods, and I wouldn't have it any other way.

EPILOGUE

10 YEARS LATER - MYRIN

Elara stood in front of our daughter, Nyura, both of their hands out before them, palms up. "Ready?" Elara asked.

We had no idea who the father was, since it felt like we could all see aspects of ourselves in Nyura, but none of us cared. She was Elara's daughter, a damn near replica of her, and we had been wrapped around her finger with the first cry she'd released.

While she was only ten years old, Nyura already had great skill with her celestial powers.

"Deep breath," Elara whispered.

Nyura took a deep breath, as deep as her little body could make.

"Envision a sun ball in your hand. Warm, but not hot. Just like the sun on your face on a warm spring day," Elara said.

Nyura bobbed her head once, her black hair with white streaks bouncing, pressed her lips together, and then a ball of sunlight appeared, hovering over her palms. The ball rotated slowly, like a planet.

Elara rested her hands on Nyura's shoulders. "Turn slowly, look towards your target, and then throw it."

My mouth dropped open, my arms fell to my sides, and I took three steps before Venali grabbed my arm and stopped me.

"Stay," he whispered without taking his eyes from the two girls we loved more than life itself.

"Ven—"

"Shush," he ordered me, his tone harsh, while the love in his eyes as he continued to stare at the girls did not waver.

I sighed and folded my arms across my chest. "I'm not cleaning shit up."

He smiled wide.

"Throw it as hard as you can and then if it doesn't go far enough, use your connection to it to push it even farther," Elara said.

Nyura nodded, turned slowly, keeping her eyes on the swirling ball, and then she lobbed it away from us and out into the ocean. With narrowed and focused eyes, she sent the ball out to a small rock formation and then released it.

The sun ball fell onto the rocks and then the light disappeared.

Nyura's lower lip trembled and she said, "I told you I couldn't—"

The rocks exploded and the shockwave knocked all of the water away from the rocks.

Ryul threw up a translucent shield, protecting us from the flying debris.

Nyura squealed and jumped up and down, pumping her arms as she did, and then did a little dance.

Elara hugged her and kissed the top of her head. "That's my girl."

"Momma, how much longer do you have?" Nyura asked, her face pressed to Elara's chest.

Elara looked over at us, tears welling in her eyes.

The seven of us hurried over, dropped to one knee in a circle around the girls, and looked at our demigoddess daughter.

"I have ninety years, baby. Plenty of time left with you," Elara whispered, tears brimming.

"Ninety years is so little in our lifetime," Nyura whispered. "Why can't I have more time with you and my fathers?"

I took Nyura's hand and rubbed the back of it. "I'm sorry, beautiful, but that is what must happen. We will return to the stars and you will rule over Minloa as queen."

She turned her little head and sniffled as she held back tears. "I'm going to miss you, though."

I pulled her into my arms and hugged her tightly. "We have a lot of time to spend together before that happens. When you're one hundred, you'll probably be tired of us and beg us to leave."

She shook her head. "No, I won't. I never want you to leave."

Elara covered her mouth with her hands and tears dripped down her face as she looked at us.

I was having a tough time keeping from tearing up myself. I hoped this child stayed as sweet as she was now.

"Hey, what about us?" Venali asked, pulled Nyura from my arms, and picked her up, cradling her against his chest. "Won't you miss me?"

She threw her arms around his neck and squeezed. "Yes."

"Even me?" Daniel asked.

Nyura leaned back, wiped her face, and looked at each of her fathers. "Every single one of you."

Daniel took Nyura and hugged her. "You're going to be the greatest queen in history."

"Hey," Elara protested.

Ryul tweaked the tip of Nyura's nose. "Even better than your momma."

"I'm standing right here," Elara said, but her smile was evidence that she was playing along.

"It wouldn't be hard," Nyura teased, looking at her mother with a wide smile.

Elara's mouth dropped open and she tickled Nyura while Daniel held her.

Nyura laughed and squealed as she was tickled.

She broke free of Daniel, only to be snatched up by Kydrus. "There is no escape for you, little princess." He tickled her more, making her laugh harder.

Then, Amrynn grabbed her and ran towards the castle. "I'll save you, my princess."

Nyura slid around Amrynn as he ran, wrapping her legs around his stomach and her arms around his neck. "Hurry, Father! They're gaining on us."

Venali teleported to them, trying to grab her from Amrynn's back, but he spun away, making Nyura shriek with laughter.

Ryul tried to grab her next, but Amrynn grabbed her arms and tossed her high up into the air, knocked Ryul's legs out from under him, and then caught her the moment she fell back down to his reach.

Elara gasped, but I wrapped my arms around her waist and held her captive. "Even after ten years you don't trust us?" I asked.

She relaxed in my arms, her body melting against mine. "She's my baby."

"As she is ours. Stop fretting." I nipped her ear and she hissed through her teeth.

"That's never going to happen," she grumbled, but leaned her head back against my shoulder and stayed with me while the others continued to run around with Nyura.

"She's going to be okay when we leave, right?" Elara asked.

"My goddess, she is going to be more than alright. I bet by the time we are preparing to leave she will have her own harem of consorts and will be begging us to leave her alone. You have no need to worry about her. She's better with her magic than you were two decades ago."

"Rude," Elara muttered, but did not try to deny it.

A group of people marched across the lands towards the castle. The person at the head of the group ran forward, closing the distance to Nyura quickly.

Elara pulled away, preparing to run for Nyura, but the newcomers beat her. With lightning quick movements, he stole Nyura from Amrynn's arms and then tossed her up into the air within a translucent bubble that held her there.

Elara let out a breath and sagged her shoulders. "I wish he wouldn't do that."

Elryd walked towards us, Nyura and the bubble hovering over his head and moving as he did.

"There you are," he said as he got to us.

The bubble popped and I caught a laughing Nyura in my arms.

"I hate that you do that," Elara grumbled, but stepped forward and hugged Elryd, a smile slipping out.

He patted her back and smiled at me. "Your little one loves it, though."

Nyura wrapped her arms around my neck and cuddled against my chest with a yawn.

She was getting to the age where she didn't want to be cuddled often, so I treasured every moment she gave me.

"Would you like to join us for dinner?" Elara asked Elryd.

He smiled and nodded. "My troops came to do some more cross training with your people. I'm sure they know the way by now."

"I'll take them," Venali called and waved at us.

"Why am I so sleepy?" Nyura asked softly.

"You expended a lot of energy to blow up those rocks," I said. "It makes you sleepy and hungry."

"Blow up rocks?" Elryd asked and looked at Elara. "She can already make the sun ball?"

Elara beamed and nodded; her pride obvious. "She can."

"I thought it had fizzled out at first," Nyura said and yawned. "Then it exploded and it was awesome."

"Come, let's get her some food so she can take a nap after her belly is full," I said and headed to the castle.

"I'm not a baby," Nyura mumbled, her eyes half-closed.

"You'll always be my baby," I whispered and kissed her cheek.

"Even when I'm one hundred?" she asked.

"Even when you're one thousand," I replied.

"How long do you live?" Kydrus asked Elryd.

I barely managed to stop myself from jumping since I hadn't heard or felt him teleport to us.

"I likely have a few hundred more years left," Elryd said. He looked from Kydrus to Elara and then to me. "Why?"

"Kydrus, will you take Nyura?" I asked.

"You're going to talk about me, aren't you?" Nyura asked as Kydrus took her.

I smiled. "Why would you think that?"

She rolled her eyes. "You're a terrible liar, father."

Kydrus teleported away with Nyura, and I turned to face Elryd. "There's something we haven't told you," I said.

He stopped walking and faced Elara and I with folded arms. "Out with it."

"I'm only here for another ninety years," Elara said. "Then my consorts and I return to the stars, becoming gods and goddesses once more."

His eyes widened and his mouth dropped open. "You're serious?"

We nodded.

Elara bent over at the waist, bowing to Elryd. "Would you please continue watching over my daughter once she becomes queen? I can watch her, but won't be able to meddle. She'll be an adult, but I would rest much easier knowing you were going to look out for her and assist her should she need it."

Elryd gripped her shoulders and straightened her. "You do not need to humble yourself to me, my friend. I would have done it without being asked. I will, of course, watch over our little Nyura. She's like a niece to me."

Elara threw her arms around Elryd and hugged him tightly. "Thank you."

He patted her back and said, "You're welcome."

Elara turned to me and smiled, her posture and smile more relaxed than I had seen her in a decade. "Let's get some food."

Elara skipped ahead and I walked beside Elryd. "Thank you," I said and looked at him.

He shook his head while smiling. "You don't need to thank me. Seriously, I would have done it no matter what. Even if you'd told me to mind my own business, I likely would have sent a spy or two to ensure she stayed safe."

I laughed and draped my arm around his shoulders, giving him a quick squeeze. "I would expect nothing less from you."

"So, when you disappear in ninety years, does that mean I get first dibs to Venali's weapons?" Elryd asked.

I laughed and said, "You'll have to take that up with the brute."

"I'm not a brute," Venali grumbled from in front of us.

I looked up and smiled. "You are, too."

He sighed. "I'm just a misunderstood teddy bear."

"I resent that statement," Daniel yelled from within the dining hall.

Elryd and I laughed and we entered the dining hall to find it full of his men and ours.

Elara and Nyura sat in the front, surrounded by some of my brothers and some of Elryd's men. The girls smiled nonstop throughout dinner and I found myself doing the same.

This was what I had always wanted. This was perfection.

As long as I could keep my girls safe and happy, I would be happy as well.

A young boy peeked out from behind one of Elryd's men, his eyes glued to Nyura.

I looked at Elryd who whistled as he looked away from me.

"Already scheming, aren't you?" I asked.

He laughed and took a bite out of a bread roll, chewed it up, and then said, "I have no idea what you're talking about."

I pointed my bread roll at him. "Just remember that we are all still here for the next ninety years, so we won't let your schemes be accomplished so easily."

He winked as he took another bite of bread.

A second boy around Nyura's age entered the room with one of Elryd's men and walked right up to her.

I looked at Elryd who shrugged with a smirk.

The boy bowed to Nyura and then held out a flower to her.

Nyura's cheeks turned bright red as she took the flower and smelled it.

I growled and heard six other growls resound around the room.

Elara rolled her eyes, whispered something in Nyura's ear, and then smirked at me.

I arched a brow, but she just continued smirking.

Nyura grabbed her plate and she and the two boys went to the far side of the room to an empty table and began talking as they ate together.

"Check. Mate," Elryd said and brushed invisible dust off his shoulders.

"Scheming elf," I grumbled, but there was no heat to it.

As long as these boys were good to her, I didn't care. Nyura deserved someone to make her happy. I just doubted they would meet our standards.

"Aren't they adorable?" Elara asked from behind me.

I hadn't seen her move, but kept from jumping as I turned to her. "You're okay with this?"

She shrugged. "They're children. She'll likely find many males to flirt with between now and when she chooses a mate."

"Or mates," Elryd said.

Elara nodded. "Yes."

"So, does that mean we can start trading for the summer?" Elryd asked.

Elara arched a brow. "Trading?"

He smiled. "I give you my boys for the summer, to learn from you and your consorts. Then the next summer you let Nyura come stay with me for the summer to learn from us."

Elara scowled a moment and then sighed. "That's likely a really good idea. It will let her experience other cultures and learn from you. And, I wouldn't mind having some more kids running around the castle."

I pulled Elara down into my lap and whispered into her ear, "There are other ways to have more kids running around the castle."

She chuckled and slid her hands down my chest. "Oh? Perhaps you should show me these ways."

"Excellent idea," Venali said, grabbed Elara, and teleported away.

"Asshole!" I yelled and stood.

"You seven are a riot," Elryd said and laughed.

"Keep an eye on Nyura?" I asked.

Elryd saluted me with his bread roll. "Yes, sir."

Kydrus set a hand on my shoulder and smiled. "Let's catch our mate and try for heir number two."

I smiled and nodded. "Let's."

We teleported to our bedroom and found Elara standing over a hogtied Venali.

"What?" I asked as I held in my laughter.

"He wasn't going to wait for you," she said and shrugged. "So, I tied him up."

I looked down at him. "Why aren't you breaking out of the ropes?"

He shrugged his shoulders. "She enjoyed having tied me up. I didn't want to break free and ruin her enjoyment."

Elara narrowed her eyes. "You can break free?"

Venali flexed and every rope broke and fell off. He stood and dusted off his body. "Yes."

She groaned. "Of course you can."

Venali tried to grab Elara, but she squealed and darted around us to the other side of the room.

"Let's make this a game," Elara said.

"A game?" Ryul asked as he and the rest of my brothers entered the room.

"Whoever is the last man standing gets first try at making heir number two," she said, smiling wickedly.

"Last man standing?" Ryul asked.

Amrynn wasted no time, knocking Ryul's legs out from under him.

Ryul landed on his side and groaned.

"Ryul's out," Elara announced.

The five of us that remained, turned and faced each other with wide smiles.

"Let the games begin!" Elara announced.

No matter what happened, these were the times I would cherish and remember the fondest. The times when everyone was smiling and laughing.

I couldn't wait to see what the next ninety years had in store for us.

ABOUT THE AUTHOR

Catherine Banks is a USA Today bestselling fantasy author who writes in several fantasy subgenres and has multiple pseudonyms. She began writing fiction at only four years old and finished her first full-length novel at the age of fifteen. She is married to her soulmate and best friend, Avery, who she has two amazing children with. After her full-time job, she reads books, plays video games, and watches anime shows and movies with her family to relax. Although she has lived in Northern California her entire life, she dreams of traveling around the world. Catherine is also C.E.O. of Turbo Kitten Industries™, a company with many hats including being a book publisher and Etsy store full of nerdy fun.

facebook.com/catherinebanksauthor

twitter.com/catherineebanks

amazon.com/author/catherinebanks

bookbub.com/authors/catherine-banks

MORE FROM CATHERINE BANKS

ADULT PARANORMAL & FANTASY ROMANCE SERIES

Zodiac Shifters Paranormal Romance Series

Centaur's Prize

Tiger Tears

Lion About

Ciara Steele Novella Series

True Faces

Barbaric Tendencies

ADULT REVERSE HAREM PARANORMAL & FANTASY ROMANCE SERIES

Her Royal Harem Series

Royally Entangled

Royally Exposed

Royally Elected

Royally Enraged

Her Royal Harem, The Complete Series

The Demon's Fair

Her Royal Harem, The Coloring Book

Wings of Vengeance Series

Of Dragons and Cruelty

Of Minotaurs and Sacrifice

Wings of Vengeance, The Complete Series

Their Fae Goddess Trilogy
Queen of the Stars

Empress of the Galaxy

Goddess of the Universe

Their Fae Goddess, Complete Trilogy

Bonds of Madness Series
Sealing the Deal

Her Super Harem Series
Lucky Strike

VELLA ADULT PARANORMAL REVERSE HAREM ROMANCE
Shark (Season One)

The Golden Alicorns (Season One)

MORE FROM CATHERINE BANKS

STANDALONE YOUNG ADULT PARANORMAL & FANTASY ROMANCE BOOKS

Monster Academy
Daughter of Lions
Lady Serra and the Draconian
Of Sky and Sea
The Last Werewolf
Sybil Deceived
An Outcast Among Wolves

STANDALONE YOUNG ADULT PARANORMAL & FANTASY REVERSE HAREM ROMANCE BOOKS

Moon Academy
Claws & Wings

STANDALONE ADULT PARANORMAL & FANTASY ROMANCE BOOKS

Dragon's Blood

Last Ama Princess

Transforming Rose

Alys of Asgard

Phoenix Possessed

Stone Heart

STANDALONE URBAN FANTASY BOOKS

The Pawn

CHILDREN'S BOOKS

Calvin's Alien Adventure

MORE FROM DAISY EMORY

The Boyfriend Deal

Their Purple Girl

ACCIDENTAL MOBSTER SERIES
Accidental Mobster
Unintentional Pirate
Suddenly Baroness
Unexpected Assassins*

LIPSTICK & LEATHER SERIES
Trinity
Alicia*

*Coming Soon